hero

a novel
by Boyd Taylor

Published by The Katherine Brown Press, Austin, Texas
KBTPress@ymail.com
Editor-in-Chief: Mindy Reed, The Authors' Assistant

Library of Congress Cataloging-in-Publishing Data
p. cm.

ISBN-13: 978-0-9894707-2-8

To Melba

Other books by Boyd Taylor

The Antelope Play
The Monkey House

PROLOGUE

The following article appeared in the April edition of the monthly magazine *This Texas*:

THE HERO OF SAN JACINTO
By D. R. Cuinn

For generations, Texas school children have been taught that Captain Sam Eben Payne was the real hero of the Battle of San Jacinto, ranking just below Sam Houston himself in the galaxy of stars of the Texas Revolution. Now it turns out that Sam Houston didn't share that view and in fact engaged in a massive cover-up to protect the reputation of Captain Payne, the man celebrated in the newspapers of the day as the man who single-handedly captured Santa Anna.

Captain Sam Payne, in case you've been out of state this election season, is the great-great-grandfather of Texas Attorney General Sam Eben Payne V, the leading candidate for Governor of Texas in this year's general election.

The received wisdom, reported to the new Republic by Houston himself is that Captain Payne was the captor of Santa Anna. Generations of Texas schoolchildren have been taught that he saw El Supremo dressed in a private's uniform and recognized him as the Mexican president and commander-in-chief; that he ran him down on horseback in the face of gunfire and delivered him to General Houston with the famous words, "Remember the Alamo! Here's the Bastard!"

We know that after recovering from his capture, Santa Anna cooper-ated with the Texans and ordered his second in command to leave Texas with the rest of the Mexican army. It was only after he had been to Washington, met with the president of the United States and was paroled to Mexico, that he resumed his bellicosity against Texas. Even then it was muted, the effect perhaps of the real events surrounding his capture.

Deep in the bowels of the Texas Archives, exists a different account of that day, written in Houston's own hand, an account so damning that Captain Payne was forced to swear to its accuracy before a Supreme Court justice. Houston threatened to make the document public if Payne ever sought public office in Texas again, even as a constable in that "God damned desert where you will spend the rest of your days." The document was to be opened only if the Hermit of West Texas, as Captain Sam was known for the rest of his eighty years, violated the terms of his agreement with Houston and returned to Austin, or sought a public role in Texas.

The desert Houston referred to was the thirty five thousand acres of West Texas land granted to Captain Payne by a grateful Republic of Texas. That land, of course, is home of the Payne Oil Field and the source of the Payne family wealth. One senses from the document that Sam Houston would not have appreciated the irony. That wealth did not come easily. Three generations of Paynes led a hard-scrabble existence on the barely arable ranch, raising a few cattle and a lot of goats. During the Great Depression it was rumored that only the family's name and its glorious ancestor allowed the present Texas Attorney General's grandfather, Sam III, to avoid foreclo-sure. Even then and through World War II, Sam III insisted that there was oil underneath the sand dunes of the Payne Ranch, and it was his persistence (some said recklessness) that finally led to the discovery of the Payne Field. For years, Sam III looked for an oil company willing to drill a test well on the ranch, before finally persuading a Midland driller named Abern to drill a wildcat. (Today, Abern Oil Company is one of the biggest independent oil and gas companies in the United States, and most of its production still comes from its Payne Ranch properties.) The first Abern well, called the Sam Eben

No. 1, showed an oil sand, but it did not produce in paying quantities. Sam III would not let Abern give up, and to the everlasting gratitude of his heirs, took a 50% working interest (responsible for his 50% of the costs and entitled to 50% of the income and not just to a one eighth royalty.) That decision meant that when the Sam Eben No. 2 well came in as a producer, the Payne family was partners with Abern and not just a landlord receiving royalties. It also meant that Sam III had to come up with his share of the large costs to develop the ranch. He exhausted his credit with the banks. Oil sold then for less than $3.00 a barrel and a well had to produce 50,000 barrels just to break even. Sam III knew the oil riches were down there, but he was cash short. Desperate, he turned to outside investors. Trading on his grandfather's fame as the Hero of San Jacinto, he brought in Hollywood promoters, and Bob Hope and Bing Crosby were soon cashing Payne Ranch royalty checks. Needing even more funds, the California promoters flew in a group of Hollywood models and starlets and photographed them on drilling rigs, working on the equipment in the altogether. It paid off. The rights of the investors ran their term, and the Payne family and Abern Oil have pumped tens of millions of barrels of oil from the Payne Ranch Field. It would not be the last time that the Payne family would trade on its illustrious forbearer. Sam IV moved to Midland and became an influential behind the scene player in Texas politics He supported the arts in West Texas by building a museum, nominally devoted to the Battle of San Jacinto, but in fact, a glorification of the Hermit of West Texas and his role in the Texas War of Independence. Sam V filmed commercials at the museum in his successful races for state senator and later, attorney general. The Hermit of West Texas played a prominent part, as did, of course, the oil millions that helped finance Sam V's campaigns.

Those days may be over, however, on account of the document discovered recently by the author in the course of research for a thesis about Houston and the early days of the Civil War. It was folded inside one of Houston's journals containing an early draft of Houston's speech of resignation on the occasion of Texas' secession from the Union. The handwriting on the document clearly appears to be Houston's. It describes what Houston calls

3

"the real events of the capture of General Santa Anna and the disgraceful conduct relating thereto of Captain Sam Payne."

The first, if not the most salacious, new information about that day concerns the attempted escape by Santa Anna. According to the document, believing that the battle was lost, Santa Anna threw on, not a private's uniform, but the dress of his mistress (finally confirmed in Houston's account to be the Texas spy Emily Morgan, a beautiful mulatto girl known as the Yellow Rose of Texas) with whom El Supremo was in flagrante delicto when the first shots were fired, and so dressed, Santa Anna ran for safety.

Even this new information would be enough to make the Houston discovery important. Confirmation of the identity of Santa Anna's noontime companion, and the account of the President of Mexico running from the battlefield dressed as a woman establish as almost incontrovertible fact what had long been rumored—that Houston had a spy in the Mexican camp, in the Mexican commander's bed, and it was her information that led him to order an attack when he did; and that Santa Anna had fled the battle under less than heroic circumstances. Both suggestions had been doubted by Texas historians and dismissed out of hand by Mexican scholars.

These revelations will not be good for Texas-Mexican relations.

What happened next is even more scandalous, is completely unexpected and may have a more immediate impact in Texas. In the upcoming gubernatorial election, a direct descendant of Captain Sam, Texas Attorney General Sam Eben Payne V, the Republican, faces a strong challenge from underdog Democrat Bob Braeswood.

The Attorney General has spent millions on TV ads calling for a "New Hero of San Jacinto" and a return to the "Spirit of the Texas Revolution." One ad shows a reenactment of the Battle of San Jacinto, starring Captain Sam and segueing neatly to the Attorney General, standing proudly before the only known statue of his great-great-grandfather, behind the courthouse in Eben Payne County.

Another ad shows the Attorney General astride his now-famous horse, Trigger V, a descendant of Roy Roger's Trigger, galloping toward the camera.

The Attorney General waves his hat and shouts "Remember the Alamo! Remember San Jacinto!"

Payne has apparently chosen to write off Hispanic voters. His campaign is aimed directly at Braeswood's blue-collar base. The question now is whether he can survive an account from Sam Houston himself, that Captain Sam not only did not capture Santa Anna, but instead, in a drunken stupor, attempted to rape what he thought was a girl fleeing the battlefield.

What's more, and perhaps even worse to many of Payne supporters, when he tore the dress off the General and realized the object of his assault was a man in disguise, he still tried to force himself on the terrified Mexican, who only then turned and ran for Houston's camp for protection, screaming, "Detén al Pervertido!"

Fortunately for the Mexican general, Houston's tent was nearby. Santa Anna ran there unobserved by anyone other than Houston's immediate staff. After the day's remarkable events, they were sworn to secrecy. Amazingly, not one of the five men aware of the day's events ever spoke publicly of them again.

The drunken Payne followed hot on the heels of Santa Anna and passed out at Houston's feet. He lay there as Santa Anna complained bitterly to Houston in Spanish about the "pervertido" and "bastardo" who had tried to rape him.

Houston had the unconscious man dragged out of sight and sent for Santa Anna's trunk. After the General had donned a proper uniform, Houston presented him to the Texas army. Needing a hero, Houston himself told his men of Santa Anna's capture and invented the famous line supposed to have been uttered by Payne, "Remember the Alamo. Here's the Bastard!"

He thus made a hero out of Payne. A shrewd judge of men, Houston used the affair to bargain with Santa Anna, not only by threatening to reveal what really happened, but also by bringing a sober but still menacing Payne into the General's presence and suggesting he might appoint Payne as Santa Anna's personal guard if an agreement wasn't reached that very day. An agreement was reached, and quickly.

That might have been the end of the affair. It would have been a lucky ending for Payne, turning infamous actions into heroism, courtesy of Houston. But Payne was not only susceptible to liquor and unnatural sex acts. He also committed a grave sin in Houston's eyes. "Puffed up" as Houston writes, by the news accounts of his bravery "and ambitious far beyond his talent." Payne quickly began to see himself as a natural leader of men, one who perhaps might even be the next president of Texas, a rival of Houston himself.

Why anyone would expect Houston to allow such impudence is hard to imagine. But Payne soon learned the magnitude of his error. Houston summoned him to the president's house and, in a private meeting, told Payne his fate. It was exile to far West Texas, where he was ordered to remain the rest of his life, albeit on land granted by the Congress of the Republic of Texas. The alternative was public exposure, humiliation and a criminal trial. Payne took the deal and moved west, never to return. A county was named after him, and he earned the sobriquet "The Hermit of West Texas" and a reputation for extreme modesty. (Another of the Payne campaign ads says, "Like his ancestor, he only talks when he has something to say. And he's talking now. It's time to save Texas again!") The Hermit never received guests, never left the county that bore his name and apparently never knew for sure what Houston had done with the affidavit he had been forced to sign. It seems that all Houston did was put it in the back of one of his journals where it lay forgotten until recently.

The Attorney General has declined comment on this article, "pending review of the libels."

Bob Braeswood's campaign also had nothing to say for publication, but his representative could be heard laughing uncontrollably at the other end of the phone line.

CHAPTER ONE

Donnie Ray Cuinn was nestled deep in his feather mattress, snuggled tight against his feather pillow, wrapped in his soft blanket, a Christmas present from his mother. Sleeping soundly and dreaming about the very blonde, unusually accommodating, and extremely elastic girl Donnie thought of as "The Acrobat." She had been in the bed with him when he went to sleep, but she was gone and the dream was replaced by extremely loud, hammering. He finally woke up enough to realize that someone was banging on his door. The hammering got even louder and more insistent.

"Cuinn? D. R. Cuinn? Are you in there?"

More pounding.

Thoughts of The Acrobat vanished, consigned to the recesses of the brain where good memories resided.

"D. R. Cuinn!" More hammering. "Answer the door!"

He lay still for a long minute, pulling the pillow over his head. He prayed for the dream to return and for the noise to go away.

It didn't work.

"Goddamn it," Donnie said, dragging himself out of the warm bed. He had been with Wesley and the girls until dawn, celebrating Donnie's long-awaited graduation. The effect of too much beer and too few aspirin hit him when he struggled to his feet. The voices were coming from outside his door.

"Hurry up, Cuinn," one said. "Peace Officers! We know you're in there. Get your ass to the door or we'll break it down."

He got his ass out of bed, a bed still warm with the imprint of The Acrobat, and got to the door, barely conscious. For no good reason, probably having to do with being only half awake, he opened the door and blinked at the Central Texas sun. It was noon in August in Austin. The sun and the heat hit him at the same time.

Two very large men in tight-fitting suits barged into his small apartment. For a second he thought he might still be asleep, but he wasn't. *These two clowns are for real.* Donnie stared at them with his first-thing-in-the-morning, before-even-his-first-cup-of-coffee brilliance.

"Huh?" he said smartly.

"Cuinn," the taller one said. "You're a mess. It's noon. Is that all you T. U. fairies do: party and flop out? You're disgusting. Put some clothes on."

Donnie looked down at himself stupidly. His head throbbed and his eyes stung and his throat was scratchy. Even so, he could tell that he was naked. He did have his soft blanket in one hand though, and he draped it over himself, toga style. Rather smartly, he decided through the haze. "Huh?" he managed again.

The tall man (Donnie thought he looked like Mount Everest) didn't seem surprised at Donnie's limited vocabulary. "You're D. R. Cuinn?" he asked. "T.U. graduate student?"

Only Aggies call The University of Texas, T.U. I should correct him, Donnie thought, then decided against it. Donnie shook his head with confusion. Of course nothing really surprised him. He had survived six years as a student at the University. He had just received his Master's Degree in Nineteenth Century American History. His thesis had been accepted. Soon he would be teaching young college freshmen, molding their mushy minds, working on his doctor's degree. *I am mature, and ready to take my rightful place in the education establishment.* He was too urbane for anything to surprise him. At the same time, he wished he were back in bed, or even better, upstairs in the café watching the daytime soaps with Lena.

"Huh?" he repeated himself.

"Well, are you?" the shorter man asked.

Donnie observed if the taller goon was Mount Everest, the shorter one was Mount Etna. If a human being could smolder, he was smoldering. He seemed, well, out of sorts.

Etna twisted one end of Donnie's makeshift toga in his beefy hand and pulled Donnie closer to his baldness. "Are you the D. R. Cuinn that's been slandering public officials?"

He grabbed back his blanket. *My mother gave me that,* he almost said, but even drowsy, he knew unexpressed thoughts seemed wiser, somehow. Instead he gulped and finally recovered the power of speech. "Are you serious? Who are you guys?"

Etna flashed a badge. "Special Investigators for the Attorney General's office. General Payne wants to talk to you. About the fucking *This Texas* and the fucking things you've been writing about him and his granddaddy. He wants to fucking see you right this fucking minute."

Even in Donnie's impaired condition, he knew what they were talking about. *Wesley Bird will not believe this.*

"Get dressed," Everest ordered. "We're driving to the Capitol to see General Payne."

Donnie pulled on a pair of jeans and a wrinkled t-shirt and stepped into his dirty sandals.

"Jesus," Etna said. "No fucking underwear? You're going to meet the Attorney General of Texas without any underwear?"

This guy really is out of sorts. Donnie went to the dresser and rummaged around until he found a pair of clean underwear. He vaguely resented their insults. Only last night, The Acrobat had told him he was cute, and Lena always said that with his sandy hair and slender build, he looked a lot like the young Robert Redford, "before the wrinkles and bad dye job." Of course, The Acrobat was drunk...and horny, and Lena was his stepmother and he could do no wrong as far as Lena was concerned. Cute or not, Sundance Kid or not, Donnie doubted that his well-practiced *Aw Shucks*, hangdog grin would work on these two.

They turned away while he put on his briefs. They guarded the door; apparently afraid Donnie was going to make a run for the border. He started to comb his hair, but they were having none of it. They half-dragged him out of his apartment and across the parking lot. His was the largest apartment at the Haven and he was proud of it, in a way. He certainly didn't believe he deserved to be dragged out of it. He was sure there was some Innkeeper's Law that prohibited that sort of thing.

Regardless, there he was, being manhandled across the stubby grass, under the giant old live oak trees that shaded the entire property, both the Haven Hotel and its adjoining Coffee Shoppe. The neon sign had once said, "Lena's" after Lena Rothschild, the proprietress and his guardian angel, but years ago all the letters other than the L had burned out, so people called the café "The L" and "Going to L" was understood by West Campus students to mean going to Lena's for some eggs and grits or maybe some chicken fried steak. It did not bother Lena enough that she ever considered replacing the letters in the sign. *Truth be known, she probably was proud of it. Sort of an Austin Weird kind of thing,* Donnie had decided.

The familiar smell of frying bacon drifted across the parking lot. It was past breakfast service, so Lupe, Lena's number one assistant and sous chef, was probably frying some more bacon for Lena's famous BLTs. Donnie could see the bread already stacked neatly in the kitchen, ready to be toasted, and the big container of Miracle Whip, ready to be spread.

Lena was probably hard at work, planning the dinner menu, an activity she took very seriously, even though, as far as Donnie could remember, the menu had never changed in all the years he had lived there. Meatloaf on Monday, Spaghetti and Meatballs on Tuesday, Swiss Steak on Wednesday, Enchiladas on Thursday, Fried Catfish on Friday, Chicken Fried Steak on Saturday, Baked Chicken and Dressing on Sunday. Lena would cook other orders on any day, but she didn't like it, and she let the customers know it. Few repeated that mistake.

Donnie glanced nervously in the direction of the café, hoping that Lena didn't see this. It was embarrassing. Besides, if she saw these guys abducting him, she might reach under the cash register for her handgun and commit felony murder.

The two men had parked in the handicapped parking space. It was clearly marked "Haven Hotel Guests Only." *Another probable violation,* Donnie thought. He considered pointing out these breaches of the law to them, but looking at Mount Etna, he decided to go quietly, as they say.

His tormentors were impatient. They shoved him into the backseat of a blue, government issue Crown Victoria. Sighing and grunting at some imagined injustice, they lowered themselves into the front seats. Mount Everest was driving and he made a point of locking the doors. An air freshener hung from the rearview mirror. It gave the inside of the car the smell of an overripe banana. Everest backed rapidly out of the parking lot and sped toward the Drag (the unofficial name for Guadalupe Street), which runs along the west side of the University of Texas campus. He hung a hard right, running the red light at the corner of Guadalupe and Twenty-Sixth Street, ignoring the students in the crosswalk who scattered with angry gestures, and Donnie imagined, creative curses. *They didn't know this was the Man or they would have been more discreet. God, I wish I had been.* Everest sped down the Drag, past the Student Union Building and the light at the West Mall, almost running another red light. Donnie lurched to one side and banged against the door.

His anxiety, not helped by the air freshener, the beer, the nachos, the smoke, the beer, *oh God, the beer,* churned his digestive system. "Could I have some more air back here?" he asked weakly.

They ignored him.

"I think I'm going to be sick."

That got Everest's attention. He slammed to a sudden stop, bouncing Donnie up and down in the back seat. "Not in my car, you're not," he snarled.

He pulled to the curb and unlocked the back right door. Donnie rolled out of the car and emptied his gut under a crepe myrtle tree trying to grow in the tiny bit of grass in front of the University Baptist Church. The tree's red flowers covered the ground and mixed nicely with the contents of Donnie's stomach.

Students hurried by, careful not to step on the crouching Donnie or his mess. Otherwise, they ignored him. *They're being non-judgmental, Donnie thought approvingly. It's the University of Texas way. Or maybe this is a common occurrence: a grad student under arrest puking in front of God's house. Wait a minute, he asked himself irrelevantly, or is it irreverently? Does the University Baptist Church even believe in God? Isn't it sort of Unitarian? He wasn't sure. I needed to Google that sometime. But not right now.*

Everett knelt beside him. "Come on then, Sonny," he said in a little softer voice.

Donnie spit one last time and crawled back into the car. The big cop handed him a Kleenex and a stick of Juicy Fruit. "You can't show up in the General's office smelling like puke," he said, opening the back windows.

The warm Texas air flowed over Donnie. He closed his eyes and tried to breathe deeply. He had heard that breathing deeply would help in situations like this. Situations like when you have been manhandled and dragged across Austin to see the most important law enforcement official in Texas, who he suspected was not going to be in a friendly mood.

CHAPTER TWO

They approached the state office complex. The Texas Attorney General's office is in one of the cereal-box buildings that frame the State Capitol. Everest guided the Crown Victoria into the parking garage and aimed for a spot marked "Attorney General Staff Only." He banged the car's bumper against the concrete barrier that protected the lime green wall.

Donnie's head bounced back and forth a few more times. Etna, who had apparently ridden with Everest before, braced himself against the dashboard. The air bag did not deploy.

Donnie shook his head, wondering if you could sue an Attorney General goon for whiplash. Etna jumped out, opened the back door and dragged Donnie out of the car by the right arm. "Easy," Donnie complained. "I only have two of those."

"Yeah," Everest agreed sympathetically. "Take it easy, Charley." They escorted him onto the garage elevator. Etna watched suspiciously, apparently confusing Donnie with one of the Manson murderers. Everest hummed the theme from *The Bridge On The River Kwai*.

Out of the elevator, onto the street, across the street to one of the Cereal Boxes, into its eerily quiet granite-clad lobby, onto another elevator, this one crowded enough that Donnie doubted even Etna would kill him there. The elevator emptied onto a working floor, full of men in dress shirts and ties and women in black skirts or pants, all scurrying from one room to another, armed with yellow legal pads and Styrofoam coffee cups.

Donnie surmised that these must be the offices where the work of the Attorney General was done. *What the hell do all these people do?* They were the People's Lawyers, so he heard. He considered screaming, "I need a lawyer! Save me!" but one look at Etna and he thought better of it.

They pushed him into a waiting room the size of a hotel lobby. A receptionist flirting with an overweight man in a checked sport coat and a pompadour haircut, looked up as they entered. Her smile disappeared. "He's expecting you," she said to Everest. She looked at Donnie with what seemed to be pity, and pushed a buzzer on her desk. The oversize door opened automatically. As the goons each took one of his arms and walked him through the door, Donnie thought he heard the receptionist say to her inamorata, "That's the poor bastard."

So, sooner than he wished, Donnie found himself in the August Presence itself. The walls of the Attorney General's office were completely paneled in dark walnut. It looked solid, not like the veneer that Lena bought for Donnie to put on the walls of his little apartment. There was a smell of furniture polish in the air. It wasn't quite as offensive as the air freshener. Donnie looked down at the thick navy blue pile carpet with a giant gold star in its center. He hoped he didn't throw up again, or if he did, that it wasn't on the star. He wouldn't want to make the Attorney General of the State of Texas angry.

Across the room, a dark figure sat hunched behind a huge oak desk, his back to them, barely visible in his high backed chair. He was facing the Capitol building, which was framed in the oversized picture window behind the desk. It took a while to approach his desk, having to cross the entire length of the room, which seemed to stretch the distance from Louisiana to New Mexico. Besides, Donnie really was in no hurry. After they arrived desk side, out of breath from the trek, Texas' third-highest elected official kept them standing there for several long minutes. This gave Donnie time to admire the back of his leather chair, on which was emblazoned the Great Seal of the State of Texas. He was suitably impressed. The man in the chair made a slow turn and Donnie recognized Texas' Supreme Lawyer himself, Attorney General Sam Eben Payne V.

Payne was a formidable politician. He had spent his twenties in the Texas House of Representatives, representing the West Texas district where the Payne family's oil wealth was concentrated. It took six years and several interventions with unimpressed professors by the Dean of the Law School himself, but Sam V. finally got a law degree from the University of Texas Law School. No one was sure how he managed to pass the bar examination. There were several theories, most involving large sums of money and proxy test takers, but pass it he did, on the third try. On the mandatory celebrity wall, beside pictures of Sam V. with the Bushes and Karl Rove, and other Republican luminaries, there he was, his younger, just as short self, staring up at Texas Supreme Court Chief Justice Liam Churchill Spencer, who is handing Sam V his license to practice law in the State of Texas. Justice Spencer is staring down at the pudgy figure with even more than his usual disdain. *This is all your fault, Judge.*

Once allowed into the club of Texas politics, dominated as it is by lawyers, and in particular lawyers from The Law School, it was a short leap though the hierarchy of Texas politics, State Senator, Agriculture Commissioner, and finally Attorney General, where he was ending his third term. In each election, he ran a Good Old Boy campaign, appealing to the Republican Party's right wing base. In his years as Attorney General, he had carefully accumulated the chits of major players, the oil companies, the insurance companies, the banks, the auto dealers. Cases had been settled, investigations had been shelved and enemies had been relentlessly pursued. When he asked those players for contributions to his race for governor, the money came in, grudgingly perhaps, but it always came in. He was probably going to win and no one wanted to be on Sam V's enemies list. He had long passed the point where he needed to put his own money into one of his campaigns. There was plenty of money to hire Al Koker, the famous Hollywood director, to come to Midland and film commercials at the San Jacinto Museum, with Sam V in the role of the Hero.

He won the Republican nomination for Governor, running away from the field and making an especially impressive showing against Betty Mann Meador, the Lieutenant Governor, who many pundits had expected to force him into a run-off. Payne had successfully ignored charges of male chauvinism arising from his remark to a crowd in Midland that he was going to hog-tie that heifer and drag her to the slaughterhouse. He also told a statewide television audience that Ms. Meador ought to remember that if rape was inevitable, she should relax and enjoy it. He told an Hispanic audience in McAllen they should vote for him because he met his wife in a Mexican restaurant. None of it seemed to matter. His opponents split the anti-Payne vote and at the end he was the Republican Party's nominee for Governor of Texas.

As Payne faced the three of them, Donnie could see that the Attorney General had a massive head and a monstrous shock of white hair, carefully coifed to look tousled. He stared at Donnie through the narrow slits of porcine eyes. The large leather chair swallowed his stout body. *He must be very short,* Donnie realized for the first time.

He did not speak. In his hand he had what Donnie recognized to be a copy of the most widely read monthly magazine in Texas, *This Texas,* where Donnie's sensational discovery had been published for all of Texas to read. Under Donnie's by-line. For which he had been paid $750 dollars. Cash. It was going to be hard to deny he had written it. A stack of newspapers lay on the desk. The headline of the one on top, the Dallas Times, probably the most influential paper in Texas, screamed, *TV Ads Say Payne Hero Ancestor A Drunken Pervert.*

A look at Payne confirmed what Donnie suspected. Payne was not pleased. Payne stared at Donnie some more. No one spoke.

Finally, Everest broke the silence. "General," he said. "This is D.R. Cuinn. We located him at his apartment in the West Campus area, just where his University records said he would be."

Donnie detected some surprise, even disappointment in Everest's voice, that Donnie had been so easy to find.

"The apartment's in a building that belongs to a Mrs. Arlene Rothschild. We haven't had time yet to do a complete check on Cuinn and his associates. His DPS is clean."

Donnie grimaced. *My associates? Wesley Bird, Jr.? Former star for the University of Texas Longhorns? Honor graduate of the McComb School of Business gainfully employed somewhere in the Dallas Metroplex working for some oil man whose name Donnie could not seem to remember just now?* He hoped he was not asked that question. Wesley Bird, whom he last saw in the company of a leggy former cheerleader and present day model, in his company's apartment at the Timeless Condominium. God knows what Wesley and she were doing right now, but Donnie was sure it was better than what Donnie was about to receive from Sam Eben Payne himself. He could not wait to tell Wesley about this.

Payne waived the goons aside. "Wait by the door. Mr. Cuinn and I are going to have a talk. He smiled shiftily at Donnie. "What do they call you, son?"

Donnie hesitated, then said in a small voice. "Don. They call me Don." *Where did that small voice come from? I can't be frightened. Am I? What can he possibly do to me?*

The Twin Peaks had retreated to the far side of the room, leaving Donnie standing in front of the desk. He went into an approximation of parade rest. After all, this man was a general.

Payne stared at him.

Donnie stared through the picture window at the Capitol Building, trying to make out the features on the Goddess of Justice, a replica which now adorned the top of the dome and whose help he really could use. The original was too corroded by auto-emitted smog to be exhibited anymore, and was stored inside, in the dark, out of the sunlight. *There's a moral there somewhere, he told himself, trying to decide how to work it into the conversation.*

The Attorney General stood and pawed through papers on the top of his desk. He tried unsuccessfully to reach a folder on Donnie's side of the desk.

Donnie watched with fascination as the Attorney General of Texas half-crawled up on the furniture and scooted the folder back to his side of the desk. He collapsed in the leather chair, breathing heavily.

Sam Eben Payne V was not only very short, but he also looked older than in his campaign pictures, and someone must have corseted him before he did those TV commercials. On his desk was a photo of him wandering through the wildflowers at the LBJ National Park, Lady Bird tucked gently under one arm. Lady Bird had a forced smile on her face, and Donnie could imagine her screaming, "Rescue me, please!" *Sort of like Santa Anna.*

One thing that did look the same about the short man was his large head and his pomaded hair. Donnie had heard that many movie stars were little men with oversized heads. Somehow it filmed well. Sam Eben Payne V filmed well, particularly with makeup to hide the pouches under his eyes and the whiskey lines that crisscrossed his Roman nose.

"So," he said at last. "You're the expert on Captain Sam Ebenezer Payne."

Donnie didn't answer, remembering from a generation of TV cop shows that he had the right to remain silent. *When will I get to make my one phone call?*

"Don, Don, Don," Payne said softly, sadly, rolling the words out in the famous West Texas accent that Donnie recognized from all Payne's television ads. "Do you know the penalty for libeling an official of the State of Texas?"

Donnie shook his head. He seriously doubted it was possible to do such a thing, or that you could say or write anything unpleasant about this man that wasn't true. But Lena Rothschild didn't raise him to act like he just fell off the famous turnip truck, so he kept quiet. He did grin though.

"You think this is funny?" Payne demanded.

Donnie stood silent, trying to keep a straight face. It did have its humorous aspects. Even the General should be able to see that.

Unfortunately, he did not. "It's not funny," Payne exploded. "When you and this subversive rag decided to libel me and my great-great-grandfather, I thought at first I would not dignify the matter with a reply. No, I chose to just ignore you." He was turning very red in the face, and his voice rose half an octave. "But I can ignore you no longer. The stakes are too great. People who would destroy our work are using you, and you, you pup, you are aiding and abetting them." He slammed his small fist down on the desk with all the force he could muster, which wasn't much.

He seems to have hurt himself though, Donnie noted with some pleasure. However, being cool, and possessing a modest instinct for self-preservation, Donnie tried not to smile. He almost succeeded. "Aiding and abetting" did sound serious, in a half-serious way, so he kept his mouth shut.

"Now, then," Payne continued, rubbing his hand gingerly and looking at it with a puzzled expression, as if wondering why it hurt. "How did it come to pass that your so-called research, done at taxpayer's expense, I might add, found its way into this disgraceful excuse for a magazine?" Payne held his copy of the magazine at arm's length, gripping it between his thumb and index finger as if it were a soiled diaper. Inexplicably, he began to whistle Texas Our Texas, the State Song of Texas, through the gap in his front teeth.

He must cap them when he's on TV, Donnie thought, *like David Letterman.* He tried to remember the words to Texas Our Texas, but they escaped him. He hoped they weren't going to sing it.

"And published on San Jacinto Day, at that," Payne sputtered. "It's a sacrilege. It's disgraceful!"

San Jacinto Day was April 21, the day of the battle featured in Donnie's article. He had not noticed that his article had been timed to coincide with the anniversary of that battle. Some schools still closed on San Jacinto Day, although with the growing number of Hispanics in the Texas population, the observance had become a lot more muted. Some Hispanics, like Cecilia Rueda Medina, the lovely Mexican girl who also lived at the Haven, ran indignant counter-celebrations on the University of Texas Mall. Donnie smiled again, thinking of Cecilia.

That drew another sharp rebuke from Texas' Attorney General. "You insolent little bastard" he yelled. "I told you to stop smiling. I am deadly serious, do you understand me?"

Donnie straightened up and stopped smiling, even if the entire episode still seemed funny. He was making mental notes of the highlights for his report to Wesley.

Payne brought him back to reality. He shook his massive head. His tousled hair stayed in the exact cemented shape. "Don, Don. I don't know what to say. I am so deeply hurt. Do you really believe that I, Sam Eben Payne V, great-great grandson of the Hero of San Jacinto, that I, that I..." he gasped for breath before continuing, "that I would ever permit this kind of libel to go unanswered or the perpetrator go unpunished?"

Actually, Payne had indeed let the article go unanswered for several months, apparently hoping it would just slink out of public consciousness and not affect his campaign. His Democratic opponent was the well known Corpus Christi labor lawyer and Texas-style liberal, Bob Braeswood. After not mentioning the article over the summer, the Braeswood attack ads had begun running constantly. They mocked Payne's own ads, with an actor playing Captain Payne but looking remarkably like his great-great grand-son, staggering out of the brush, drunk and panting after a fleeing figure in a skirt.

Donnie wanted to say they're just TV ads, but he followed his first instincts and did not speak. He waited and waited. *You do have the right to remain silent, Donnie reminded himself again. It can't be libel if it's true, can it?* Donnie had seen Sam Houston's handwritten account of that day with his own eyes.

Payne had a Houston newspaper in his hand. "Listen to this," he shouted. "*Ads Correct. Payne Not Qualified to be Governor.* Not quali-fied? I was bred and reared to be Governor. I am genetically obliged to be Governor." He rose to his full minimal height and struck a pose that had gone out with high school declaimers seventy-five years ago. "My roots, my family, my heritage, my very genes demand that I be governor . . . whether I choose the office or not. And I do not choose it; the office chooses me."

The Democrats' ads were hilarious, Donnie thought. He had no idea they had damaged Payne so much. They must have. *Otherwise, why am I here?*

Payne sank back into his chair, almost disappearing from view. He sighed wearily. "Everywhere I go, this piss-ant article of yours and your pinko friends is thrown up in my face. 'He's a liar,' Braeswood says down in Houston. That Commie tells my supporters down there, 'You may not agree with me on every issue, but at least I'm honest. A man who'd lie about his granddaddy will lie about anything!' "

Payne's face became watermelon red.

Donnie noticed it with some concern. The way things were going, if Payne died on the spot, Donnie would probably be indicted as an accessory. *It might be worth it, he decided.*

"That Commie," Payne repeated hoarsely. "Labor union tool. Murderer of unborn children." He regained his breath and his color faded a little, to a burnt orange closely matching a faded Texas Longhorn sweatshirt. He stared at Donnie, gasping for breath.

Donnie shifted uneasily. Unfortunately, there was no place to run. *I'm sure I could outrun him,* Donnie thought. *Maybe a few times around the football field of an office would do him in.*

"All because of you and this, this piece of garbage." He threw the magazine at Donnie. His aim wasn't very good, and *This Texas* hit the stack of newspapers on his desk, scattering them in all directions. "Garbage. Manure," he said, softer now, apparently exhausted. He sighed deeply. He propped his lizard-skin boots with the extra high heels on his desk. He peered at Donnie evilly between his little feet. "This could cost me the election, do you realize that? I've already had to withdraw my TV ads. I paid a fortune to have them directed by that Hollywood fairy. Cost millions. Now they're worthless. They just remind people of your goddam article."

Donnie shook his head unbelievingly. He knew that the election was close, but the idea that an article by Donnie Cuinn could cost anyone an election seemed absurd. *Of course, this is Texas.*

The Attorney General glared up at Donnie, wiggling the toes of his boots. "Now, here's what you're going to do, boy. You are going to renounce this article. You are going to admit that your research was, shall we say, flawed, that you invented these slanders of the Captor of Santa Anna, that you lied to *This Texas*, and that you owe me an apology, all in writing and notarized. Get a notary in here," he shouted at the goons at the door.

He fumbled through the papers on his desk and found a folder from which he extracted a typed document. He shoved it across the desk. "Sign that."

Donnie picked up the document and read it:

"Before me, the undersigned authority in and for The State of Texas, personally appeared Donald R. Cuinn, who on his oath avows and states that he is the author of the attached article; that such article is a fabrication; that he knowingly misstated the article to be true; that the documentation he claims in the article does not exist; and that he retracts all the allegations in such article about the character or heroism of Captain Sam Eben Payne, the Hero of San Jacinto."

Several seconds passed. Donnie didn't say anything. It was impossible anyway. It was all too absurd. "You're not serious?" he finally managed.

"What?" the State of Texas' highest law official demanded.

"Mr. Payne," he began, not smiling now.

"General Payne."

"I'm sorry if the article upset you."

Payne snorted his disbelief.

"I didn't intend it to. But I can't retract it. It's accurate. And I'm sure not going to sign something that says I'm a liar."

Payne stared at him, as if shocked beyond belief that Donnie was refusing to do what he demanded. He sighed, as if making a great concession. "All right, then. Just sign a statement that you thought the documents were authentic, but you now know they are forgeries." He leafed through the folder and came up with a second document.

An alternative truth, Donnie thought. He read through the document. It was a little better, but not much. It said in effect that Donnie was a gullible idiot. *That might be true, but I'm not going to sign a paper admitting it,* he thought.

"You're young." Payne's voice was smarmy now. "Nobody will care."

Donnie shook his head. "No. I can't do that. Besides, the documents are in the Archives. Anybody can look at them."

Payne looked up slyly. Donnie's protest didn't seem to faze him. "You let me worry about the Archives. This isn't a game, boy. This could determine the next Governor of Texas. Maybe even a future President of the United States. Who forged that paper? Admit it and it'll go easier on you."

Donnie braced himself. *Here goes.* "No, sir," he finally said.

"What did you say, boy?" Payne demanded.

"No," he repeated. "The document's not a forgery. I found it in the Archives, just like I wrote."

Payne shook his massive head in disgust. "My staff is meeting with the State Archivist at this very minute. I predict he'll agree we have a clever little forgery on our hands."

Payne picked up another folder and shook it in Donnie's face. "This is your file, Don. We know everything there is to know about you. Yessiree, Bob, all about your scummy little life." He opened the folder and peered down at it. "Let's see here. Taken you six years to get through the University. Now twenty-eight years old. Finally ready to start your career, I guess. Let's see, where is that application?" With a triumphant sneer he pulled a document out of the folder and showed it to Donnie.

With the shock of recognition, Donnie saw what it was. "Where did you get that?" he asked.

"From the head of the History Department of the University of Texas," Payne replied. "Unlike you, he was happy to cooperate in my investigation." He thumbed through the sheets. "I see you've applied for a teaching fellowship at two of our fine state universities."

He was right. Donnie's faculty advisor said that with his M.A. and his grades and his thesis, and now the *This Texas* article, Donnie was a strong candidate for one of two or three openings in the doctoral program at UT or at Texas A&M.

"I don't believe I would count on that, if I was you, Don. Not so long as you've got this investigation hanging over you."

Now he had Donnie's attention. He needed a job. Bad! Lena had given him free rent and all the café food he could eat, for his entire life.

She'd be a bit disappointed to hear it could go on indefinitely. She was seventy-five, and had often expressed a desire to see Donnie employed prior to her own relocation across the street to the Lincoln Washburn Funeral Home.

"Don't count on any job in this state, or in any other university. I have good friends throughout this entire country. Nobody will want to hire a fabricator and slanderer. Some kind of academic standard against it, I guess." He shuffled through the papers searching for something. He gave up and brushed them off the desk. They fluttered to the floor.

"Are you serious?" Donnie managed to say. "You'd black-ball me?"

"In a West Texas minute. Come on, Don," he said plaintively, "work with me here. You don't need all this trouble," he said with an oily approximation of sweetness. "Admit it, sign the statement, and we can part here on good terms. I'll even speak to the dean about your application. I can promise you that everything will be forgiven, and you'll get one of those positions you want so bad."

Maybe later he would think of it as bravado or bad judgment, but it seemed the only thing to do. Donnie pulled himself sharply to attention and repeated the mantra. *"No, sir." He wants me to swear to a lie, Donnie thought. That doesn't necessarily make it a bad idea. But not for Payne. No. Not ever. No, sir.* Lena would just have to put off her journey to the funeral home a while longer.

Payne flipped through the folder again. "It says here that your tuition is paid by a couple by the name of Rothschild. Is that right? Why do you go by the name of Cuinn?"

"It's my name. The Rothschilds have been like parents to me."

"It also says that these Rothschilds are a couple of left-wing agitators. That true? It would explain a lot."

Donny laughed. "That's crazy. They aren't political at all. Maybe they attended a Democratic precinct convention."

"And that she owns a flea-bag hotel by the campus and he's a poetry professor. Why am I not surprised?"

Donnie spoke up, not close to smiling now. "They have nothing to do with this, nothing at all."

Payne smiled meanly. "Oh, but they do. They've been supporting a shameless libeler and now they'll have to pay for it. I'm not sure how, but you can be sure that they'll pay. Just like you. So think carefully about what you're doing."

"Leave them out of this, please."

"Not so funny now, is it, boy? Just sign the statement and they can go on like before. Otherwise, I can't promise anything. No, wait. I can promise something. I promise them trouble…lots of trouble."

Payne had gone too far. Threatening Lena and Papa, the two people to whom Donnie owed everything, was too much. *I'll never give in to this blustering little man. Not today, not ever.* He stared at Payne, then spoke. "You know, *General,* if it was just me and my career you threatened, I might have given in. Why fight? If the people of Texas elect you Governor, I guess they deserve you. But when you bring the Rothschilds into it, I can see you for who you really are. You're just as cowardly as your great-great grandfather. No. My article's true. You've proved that to me just now. I'll never take back a word of it and I hope you rot in Hell."

Payne shook his head with what seemed like genuine regret. "Brave talk, boy, but talk is just talk. All right, then, you refuse to cooperate. My only recourse is to make sure that trash like you do not sully the halls of any educational institution in this state. I owe our young people that much. You will regret this lie for a long time."

He motioned to the goons still standing guard at the door, a terrified looking little man between them. Donnie assumed he was the notary public who was there to witness Donnie's oath.

"Get him out of my sight." Payne swiveled his chair and returned to facing the window.

CHAPTER THREE

Escorted out of the building, with no offer of a ride home, Donnie's head reeled. He had no idea what to do next. He found himself in the Capitol Rotunda. Somehow, he had made it through security, despite looking like he had spent the night at the homeless camp on Waller Creek. He wandered around, past the pictures of Texas governors, still dazed. A buzzing sound in the distance came closer. Then louder, surrounding him! For a moment he thought he was being attacked by a swarm of bees.

"And here we can see more of the important people who have been governors of Texas. How many women have been governor, does anyone know? "

The buzzing died down.

"Two, that's right. Does anyone know who they were?"

Children's voices. "Ann Richards."

"Very good. And before her, Miriam Ferguson, back before any of us were even born. See if you can find their pictures."

The buzzing started again, back at full volume.

Donnie was surrounded by children, laughing and giggling, then drawing away, frightened when they saw him. His eyes met those of their tour guide. She looked startled. "Come this way, children. Come with me. Hurry. There's something down here I want to show you." She herded her flock away from Donnie. He imagined how deranged he must look to her. *Surely I'm not the first crazy man she's run into in the Capitol…. Maybe even the Attorney General.*

He found himself standing in front of the picture of the Aggie governor with the carefully moussed hair. Next to him was a picture of the president's son who presided over the hunt for WMDs in Iraq, where one of Donnie's high school classmates was killed. Those two were bad enough. But Payne V's picture on that wall? It made Donnie puke. He barely made it to the toilet, where he vomited into the white porcelain toilet. Kneeling there, he promised: *You'll never be governor of Texas. Not if I have any thing to do with it. Never!*

Wobbly, he grasped the edge of the toilet bowl with both hands and forced himself to stand. He flushed the remnants of last night's partying and looked at himself in the mirror. *What a mess.* Even so, for the first time in a long time, maybe since Dorrie Louise left and he made him cope by himself with that, he felt anger, his lifetime of practiced placidity abruptly eliminated. He had taught himself to accept the world around him, making a point of not worrying about tomorrow, or even that afternoon, determined not to care. This was different, and it surprised him how good it felt. The anger at Payne surged through him. It might be hate, but even so, he felt purpose.

He rinsed his mouth, washed his face and brushed down his hair. He straightened his clothes as best as he could. He looked again at his reflection in the mirror. Nothing he could do about his clothes or his unshaved face; he blew into his palm…or Jesus, my breath. Even so, he promoted himself from homeless child molester to fine arts major. Maybe he wouldn't frighten any more little children. *Where to start?* He had to see Wesley, of course, but first he needed to go to the Archives. He needed to see the Houston document one more time. He hurried past the guide and her tour group. "Sorry," he said to her. "I'm really sorry."

He paused again in the Rotunda in front of the Elisabet Ney statue of Sam Houston. The German sculptress had caught the resolve in Houston's eyes. The man who won Texas its independence, who took the Republic of Texas into the Union, who opposed secession as a foolhardy act when most of his fellow Texans wanted it, that man would not shrink from exiling Sam Payne to the desert of West Texas. The Ney statue of Stephan F. Austin, the Father of Texas, was on the other side of the doorway. Austin seemed uneasy in Houston's company, John Adams destined to spend eternity across from Andrew Jackson. He saluted them both.

He smiled to himself when he thought about Elisabet Ney. In the early nineteen hundreds, the German artist had left her husband in Hempstead and come to Austin to work. She built the little castle on Forty Fourth Street, on the outskirts of Hyde Park, and held court with the Austin intelligentsia of the day. Ever since her death, the studio had been carefully preserved as a museum. Its garden was a favorite venue for weddings and fund-raisers. At the time, *Wesley was dating a gorgeous Kappa. What the fuck was her name?* Just another of Wesley's conquests. Whatever her name, she and her sorority sister were volunteer docents at the Ney Museum. The girls were working a fund-raiser at the Museum, so naturally Wesley volunteered that he and Donnie would tend bar.

"Work for free?" Donnie asked.

"It's for charity." Wesley winked. "Besides, I promise you that we'll get compensated." They mixed the drinks much too strong, enjoying the result. Dinner was late and the party got noisier and the bids at the auction higher than the sponsors had dared hope. They helped the girls pour wine, strolling among the long tables that the caterer had arranged in the garden, under strands of twinkling silver lights. They watched Austin's arts community eat their chicken crepes and mesclun salad, drink the donated wine and listen to a soprano from the Butler Music School sing Verdi arias. When the party ended, the caterer's crew restored the garden to its serene quietness and packed up the tables and chairs. The slim caterer had been thrilled to have Wesley working his party. He could hardly take his eyes off the All-American football star. He touched Wesley on the arm and asked if he was free for an event the following week. He left, disappointed but still hopeful after Wesley's diplomatic refusal.

The four of them alone, Wesley and Donnie helped the two girls set everything else right. While they were working, Wesley brought out a half case of Becker *Prairie Rotie* that he had hidden beneath Ney's plaster cast of Mad King Ludwig II of Bavaria. Later, upstairs, drinking wine with his

Kappa, he could hear the sounds of lovemaking downstairs. Donnie smiled at the girl and poured them both some more wine.

She had made it clear to Donnie that this wasn't a date. That was all right with Donnie. He would like to have slept with her of course, but he had been on enough double dates with Wesley to know that sometimes it happened and sometimes it didn't. He was all right with that. He wasn't like Wesley. *Who was?* Wesley approached every girl he met with certainty they would fuck, unless he chose not to for some reason, such as not getting in Donnie's way, or because of an emergency phone call from a coach or from some other girl. Incredibly to Donnie, Wesley's certainty was justified. Donnie could think of only two or three girls in the years he and Wesley had been friends, when Wesley offered sex to a girl and she turned the offer down. Maybe there were more, but Donnie doubted it.

Thinking about that night, Donnie remembered how good it was, talking to the girl, laughing and joking and enjoying the wine. And the other nights, when he and a girl connected in the right way, and they ended up in bed. *I had been content, hadn't I? Maybe even happy? he wondered. Why did I have to screw it up?*

The guard at the south exit of the Capitol seemed happy to see Donnie leave. He took his time going across the Capitol grounds to the Archives Building. He could see the top of the Greek Revival building. He had loved his time in there. But now he could hardly make himself go in. *What if I did miss something?* What if it was obvious the Houston paper was a fake? Would he have noticed? *Of course.* Unless he was so caught up in the excitement of his discovery that he didn't pay attention to something any real scholar, any serious researcher, would have seen? Did I?

He stopped at the reconstructed fountain on the south lawn and drank deeply from the cold artesian water. Its sulphur bitterness almost killed the taste of his vomit in his mouth. He couldn't put it off any longer. He strode purposefully across the east lawn, across the street, up the steps of the Archives. To the left there were still genealogy researchers hunched over the microfilm readers, despite almost everything being online now.

Force of habit, he supposed. He pushed open the glass doors and went into the Archives. He didn't have his researcher's card, but he hoped the clerk behind the desk would remember him. He did.

"Oh, hi," the clerk said. He brushed his shaved head and looked around nervously. No one else was nearby.

"Don Cuinn," Donnie said with a smile. "Remember me?"

"Of course. Everybody here remembers you. You've made us famous."

Donnie smiled ruefully. "I don't have my card, but I really need to see those Houston documents I looked at last time. Can you do that for me?"

The clerk shook his head. "I'm really sorry, but your privileges have been revoked."

"Revoked? What do you mean?"

"Revoked. Cancelled. Banned. You're persona non grata.

Donnie tried to hide his surprise. He grinned his shy grin, the one that usually worked with strangers. "I am not *persona non grata*. I've always been *persona grata*." He leaned over the desk and whispered conspiratorially. "I really need to see the papers. Just for a second."

"I'm sorry. I really am. But it doesn't matter whether you're banned or not."

"Why not?"

"They're gone."

"Gone? What do you mean, gone?"

"The Attorney General's office sent lawyers over here this morning with some kind of legal document and they hauled all the Houston papers out of here. They're gone." He patted Donnie on the arm and said softly, "I'm sorry. It was a hoot of an article."

Stunned, Donnie stumbled out of the building into the bright sunlight. He had to talk to Wesley. *Wesley always has a plan. He'll know what to do.* Donnie wasn't sure he believed that.

Wesley was staying at the Timeless, Austin's newest and tallest condominium, overlooking Lady Bird Lake in downtown Austin. Donnie looked back at the Attorney General's offices, looming high above the Capitol building itself. He imagined the investigators up there, pawing over the Houston papers. He wondered if the Archives staff required them to put on protective gloves before they let them handle the documents. *Probably not.* Most of Donnie's research had been in the Houston collection in the city on the bayou named after the great man and at the research center near Liberty, Texas. He had only used the State Archives for a few weeks at the end of his year's work. It hadn't been absolutely necessary, just a few loose ends to tie up, and then, bingo, there was the document, wrapped in oil cloth, stuck in the back of one of Houston's buckram bound journals. *All this trouble…just by accident.*

Donnie was torn between fear of Payne's threats and pride in how he had stood up to him. He could hardly wait to tell Wesley the story. Wesley would know if the threats were real, or if the whole thing was some sort of comic opera. Between them, they'd figure out how to keep Payne from becoming governor.

He made his way south on Congress, through the crowds. The lunch hour was ending and the sidewalks were crowded with lawyers, legal aides, paralegals, court reporters, bailiffs, judges, lobbyists, and the occasional State employee. Congress Avenue had once been the proud boulevard of Texas, wide enough for six cars abreast plus a streetcar. It had been lined with shops and restaurants of every variety. Then for fifty years the street decayed, leaving little except offices sheltering the ravenous legal octopus that fed on State business, the restored Paramount Theater, pressed into service for semi-annual revivals of *Greater Tuna*, and one or two restaurants that spilled out onto the sidewalk. During the long decline of downtown, retail shops had either been boarded up or converted to downscale stores. In the1990s, however, there was a downtown renaissance of a sort, with Austin trying to copy Seattle's Smart Growth. Austin's bloated city bureaucracy was forced to permit downtown lofts and restaurants and unconventional offices to accommodate the city's growing high tech industry. State and private workers thronged to the new eateries and shops before returning to their cubicles.

Town Lake, renamed Lady Bird Lake on the theory that everything in Austin ought to be named after Lady Bird Johnson, was a cool blue stream that marked the south boundary of downtown Austin. Donnie headed west on Cesar Chavez Avenue, or, as older Austinites called it, First Street, along the lake to the Timeless. It was definitely an upscale location, directly across the street from the lake and its popular jogging trails. He made his way past City Hall, a perplexing structure of odd shape with a seldom used public plaza in its center and poorly planned retail spaces on its first level.

Donnie didn't fit in with the legal crowd passing in and out of City Hall, being unshaven, bleary-eyed and dressed in t-shirt, jeans and sandals. *I should not be walking in these sandals,* he thought. He could feel a blister forming on his heel. On the other hand, he might have passed for an Austin real estate mogul or the young founder of a new software company wanting to make its initial public offering.

His object, though, was different from the rest of the crowd. No lunch to dawdle over, no deal to close or case to settle, no gubernatorial appointment to lobby for. No, his only purpose was to rouse Wesley Bird, Jr. from his bed of pleasure with Cindy Patson and decide whether to put a curse on him for placing him in the path of Sam Eben Payne's genetically ordained race for Governor of Texas.

Wesley had got him into this mess. After Donnie found the Payne papers in the Archives, he had laughed about it with Wesley. Wesley introduced him to his former teammate, Stu Short, Managing Editor of *This Texas* magazine. Stu offered him $750 for an article about his discovery and Donnie had decided it was a great opportunity. *That might have been a mistake,* Donnie thought ruefully. If any of those things had not happened, he wouldn't have the Attorney General of Texas as his mortal enemy.

Donnie stopped outside the Timeless and tried to raise Wesley on his cell phone, but he was shunted off to voice mail. Text messages were not received either. He decided to go up to the apartment, but he was stopped in the Timeless lobby by the concierge.

"Hi, Geraldo," Donnie said brightly. "Remember me? I'm a friend of Wesley Bird."

If Geraldo recognized Donnie, he chose not to admit it. "Mr. Bird asked not to be disturbed."

Donnie knew what that meant. "It's really important. Can you call him on the house phone? His cell must be out of order."

Geraldo declined.

Donnie tried to remember the name of Wesley's boss. It came to him. "Call and tell him that I've got a message from Sawbucks Banjo."

Even Geraldo seemed impressed by the invocation of the famous Dallas oilman. He picked up the phone and whispered quietly into it. After a moment, he handed the phone to Donnie. "He's on the line," he said, "But I don't think he's happy." He turned and went into the alcove behind the front desk. But he stayed in earshot, Donnie noticed.

"Oh, come on, Crud," Wesley said when Donnie identified himself. "I'm busy here. No fair using Sawbucks' name."

Donnie could hear Cindy calling huskily. "Come back to bed, honey."

As far as Donnie knew, Wesley had never refused an invitation like that in his entire life. It irritated Donnie a little when he thought about how many times that must have happened to Wesley Bird, Jr., who was six foot seven, and had played tight end at about two hundred thirty pounds of lean hard muscle and two percent body fat. Blond, with a square jaw and brilliant white teeth, Wesley was still in good shape, despite a little evidence of the effect of the good life on his midsection.

Several minutes later, after Donnie breathlessly explained what happened at the Attorney General's office, Wesley laughed. "Imagine, the Attorney General of Texas and my friend D. Ray Cuinn. I'm proud of you."

"We have to stop him, Wesley. I want to beat that bastard. More than anything in my life."

It sounded like Wesley was struggling against Cindy's ever more urgent entreaties, but that his heart wasn't in the battle. "And we will, Donnie. We will. Now, I'll be over first thing tomorrow. Did you know we can sit in the Jacuzzi up here and watch the bats? Cindy loves to watch those damn bats, don't you, sweetheart?"

Cindy's giggle carried over the phone.

"Wesley," Donnie interrupted impatiently, "just for a minute, can you be serious? Payne says he's going to ruin my career."

"You've got a career?"

Donnie ignored the comment. "Plus, he says he's going after Lena and Papa. I think he means it. I hate that bastard"

"Now quit that, Cindy. D. Ray needs my advice." Wesley returned part of his attention to the phone. "Payne's just pissed because he's losing the election. Don't worry. We've got him on the run. You did good, son. Go home and spend some time with your little senorita."

Donnie sighed. "I told you last night. Cecilia won't even talk to me. She's upset about the article. That's another thing I can thank you for."

"Oh, that's right. She says you defamed the entire Latino population of Texas, right?"

Donnie didn't answer.

"Well, she'll probably come around."

Donnie didn't like the word 'probably.' The sound of Cindy doing something immoral to Wesley was all too clear over the phone.

"If she doesn't, there's plenty of pepper pussy around. I'll find you some."

"You are a real prick, Wesley, you know that?"

"Takes one to know one, Crud. Apologize to her. Tell her you'll expose white male racism in your next article. She'll eat that up. Speaking of which, you'll just have to excuse me now…Oh, sweetheart, *chupame mi pajarito.*"

"Does she even know what that means?"

"Hmm." Wesley moaned happily. "I guess so. She's doing it."

Wesley hung up, leaving Donnie standing in the lobby of the Timeless. After the useless ten minutes of pleading with Wesley, he handed the phone back to the concierge, who shook his head as if to say that he knew all along that Donnie was an interloper, not entitled to enter his lobby.

CHAPTER FOUR

Donnie knew he wouldn't see Wesley before the next day, if then. If watching the bats made Cindy even hornier, and that was not easy to imagine, Wesley would stay there with her, watching the bats, as long as it worked. *When did the bats become such a tourist attraction, anyway?* he wondered. Every night at sunset, a million and a half of the little bastards flew out in dark clouds, feeding on Austin's bumper crops of mosquitoes. Watching the bats leave the bridge was on the to-do list for locals and visitors alike, part of the well-advertised campaign to Keep Austin Weird.

"You notice, D. Ray," Wesley said, "that the people who want to keep Austin Weird are the Chamber of Commerce merchant types. It's all hype, all business, you see?" Obviously, Wesley certainly did not considered batwatching cool (and Wesley's judgment of cool or not cool was binding on Donnie and all other ordinary mortals). Many a time, he and Donnie sat under the covered porch at the grill across the lake from the bridge, laughing at the picnickers as they spread their food on the grass under the bat's nightly flight path.

Wesley would laugh, "Those poor bastards don't even realize they're eating bat shit with their potato salad."

"Look at them on the bridge." Donnie pointed with his beer bottle at the crowd, wiping droppings off their shoes, and sidestepping the occasional dead baby bat. A few smarter ones huddled under umbrellas, peeking out at the swarm of bats flying from under the bridge.

The bats came north from Mexico in March. Back in 1980, when it was still the Congress Avenue Bridge, connecting north and south

Congress Avenue over Town Lake, and not the politically correct Ann Richards Bridge, over Lady Bird Lake, engineers renovated the bridge and for good engineering reasons, never well explained, designed deep crevices in its underside. Those narrow openings apparently were desirable bat maternity wards, and over the next few years, the largest urban bat colony in North America established itself under the bridge. The mother bats delivered their young and fed them until they were able to fend for themselves and then the colony departed for Mexico for the winter. To fuel this enterprise, the bats consumed tons of insects every evening, and brought impressive cash to the many businesses that profited from the bats. The packed bars and restaurants, the two river boats crowded with tourists on sunset cruises, the canoe rental business at the foot of the bridge—to all of them, the bats were a Godsend, messy perhaps, but well worth the occasional rabies scare.

Wesley may have not considered bat-watching cool, but when Cindy and Anna Kaye, her roommate, wanted to see them up-close, he found a way to convert it into a Wesley-acceptable event, fueled with alcohol and sex.

So it was that Donnie found himself with Anna Kaye, always known thereafter as "The Acrobat," in a canoe, far enough downstream from the bridge to avoid fallout. They floated alongside Wesley and Cindy's canoe, sharing wine and cheese slices that the girls brought from Central Market. By the time the bats had flown off to look for their dinner, the sun had set and the lake was dark. The tour boats passed them in the blackness, heading back to their dock on the other side of the lake. Their waves rocked the canoes gently in the warm night air. Wesley took an oar and guided his canoe into the center of the lake, out of sight. Donnie could hear Cindy's voice, carrying over the water. Donnie reached over and took Anna Kaye's arm. He stood shakily in the rocking canoe, intending to move beside her. The canoe swayed beneath his feet.

"Don't try it, Donnie. We'll capsize."

"I can do it." He got on his knees and tried to crawl toward her, but the canoe rocked from side to side.

"Sit back. I'll come over there."

"I can do it," he repeated, a little annoyed now.

"Of course you can. But I'm the one who's an All Big 12 volleyball player. Sit back down and I'll come to you."

No arguing with that. The big blond pulled her shirt over her head, shaking her hair, and then pulled her shorts off her long legs. Donnie could barely make her out in the dark, but he saw enough. He squirmed out of his shorts and watched her. With a sure move, amazingly quick for such a big girl, she was at his end of the canoe, straddling him.

"Now you be still," she ordered.

Of course that was impossible and it was only a minute before he flipped the canoe and they found themselves in the water. It was only waist deep, but their clothes and the canoe were floating away on the current.

"Oh shit," The Acrobat said. She dived into the murky water and swam with long measured strokes, easily catching up with the canoe. Donnie watched the moonlight reflect off her body. Swimming with one arm, she pushed the canoe back to where Donnie was shivering. Sloshing across the muddy lakebed, they managed to pull the canoe onshore. They spread their clothes out to dry on the bushes and found a spot for their damp beach towels. Donnie made love to The Acrobat many times after that, but nothing compared to that first time, by the lake, not far, he discovered later, from the hobo camp where Waller Creek emptied into the lake.

Memories of The Acrobat did nothing to solve the problem he had now. He decided to take the bus home and think about what to do next. He walked half way to the bus stop before he remembered he had left home with no money and no billfold. No UT I.D. that would have gotten him a free ride on the bus. Nothing. He doubted that Geraldo would lend him the bus fare. He took comfort in Wesley's reaction. Together they would figure out what to do about Payne. He was still angry, furious in fact, but he didn't have any socks on, and the pain from the blister forming on his left heel interfered with his focus a little..

He decided to walk home. Decided was another way of saying he had no choice but to walk home. *I'm not down to panhandling yet*, he told himself, but he knew with Payne as an enemy, the day might not be far away. He could see himself at the corner of Ben White and I-35 with a cardboard sign reading, *Will Do History Paper For Food.*

Wishing for a handful of aspirin, Donnie started the long trek to the University of Texas campus and home. On the off chance he might spot someone in Whole Foods who would give him a ride home, he decided to walk down to Lamar Boulevard and then home from there, The clear air helped his headache, and by the time he had walked the dozen blocks to the natural food superstore on Lamar, he felt well enough to stop for a coffee and a bran muffin. The place was filled with slender women in their slim jeans and short blouses, pushing children in Peg Perego strollers. A couple he noticed had twins in the Aria. One guy had a baby in one side of the Aria with a Pomeranian in the other seat.

He stood in line, goods in his hand and not a cent in the pocket of his torn jeans. Once again, he had forgotten that he was penniless. That dawned on him just as he reached the register.

"I'm sorry," he told the cashier, or as Whole Foods insists, "associate." She wore non-sweatshop jeans and a recycled cardboard cap. "I seem to have forgotten my billfold. I'll just put these back."

She looked at him brightly. The sun reflected off the "Save the Barton Creek Salamander" badge on her faded blue shirt, which in turn was stretched tight across her ample bosom. "Oh, don't worry," she said in typical Austin fashion. "It's only two dollars forty. The company can afford it."

This so beats panhandling, he thought. If he'd been a business major, he probably would have been required by the Business School Code of Ethical Behavior to report the girl to her manager. *Thank God history majors have no scruples.* He thanked the girl profusely, grabbed his coffee and muffin before she could change her mind, and took a last look at her breasts.

He sat at one of the picnic tables on the patio. He ate the muffin, inhaled the French Roast coffee deliberately, and thought about what had happened. *Maybe I'm putting too much faith in Wesley, but Wesley is my best friend...the only really close friend I've ever had...as much an older brother as anything else...although I've never had a brother and so I can't be sure.*

For some inexplicable reason, Wesley had taken Donnie under his wing in Spanish 411. Wesley was a good student, perhaps the only member of the football team ever to take an advanced Spanish course. Donnie helped him with his Spanish grammar and Wesley taught Donnie the Mexican slang he had picked up as a ranch hand's son in South Texas.

He also helped Donnie with his social life. He took pleasure in instructing Donnie in the mores of University of Texas dating and bedding, subjects in which Wesley was an expert and Donnie was barely an amateur, if on the roster at all. Wesley would often insist that his date find a sorority sister for Donnie so they could double date. Donnie's date usually couldn't quite hide her disappointment that she was with him instead of with Wesley, but that didn't stop Donnie from taking advantage of his famous friend's generosity. They all basked in Wesley's super nova, and the girls he arranged for Donnie turned out to be either smart, or pretty, or willing. Seldom was a girl all three. Donnie knew he was lucky to get two out of three.

At least that was true until Cindy introduced him to Anna Kaye Nordstrom, the All-American outside hitter on the University's national champion volleyball team. With the physique and blond good looks of a Nordic queen, she had such versatility in bed, not to mention a rocking canoe, that to Donnie she was The Acrobat. After graduation, she became an event planner for the Austin Convention Center. Anna Kaye, or A.K., as Wesley called her, or The Acrobat, as Donnie thought of her, was in and out of Donnie's life and his bed. He knew he had Wesley to thank for that. Although she really did seem fond of Donnie, after all, The Acrobat had bigger fish to fry than a poor history grad student.

Wesley had been the difference for Donnie during the two years before the football star graduated. The parties, the drinking, the inside jokes, the girls, made Donnie's life seem like a continuous road trip. Before

Wesley graduated to the world of high finance, he led the protected life of a starting athlete at the University of Texas. He had a well-furnished apartment in Hyde Park, north of the campus, as well as a new leased car every season. Donnie did not ask where the perks came from, but he imagined they came from alums through some byzantine process that technically complied with NCAA rules.

After they took their dates back home, Wesley and Donnie would spend the early morning hours riding around Austin in Wesley's car and talking about their pasts and the future. Wesley was adamant about one thing. A girl never spent the night at his apartment. "I am not going to wake up in the morning and see some beauty queen without her makeup on, acting all domestic, making me breakfast or hanging up my clothes. Besides," he laughed to Donnie, "it's the gentlemanly thing to do, isn't it, to take them home?"

He and Wesley would get a six-pack and drive up to Coyote Hill, a favorite place to drink beer and tell each other things they never told anyone else. Coyote Hill was an outcrop of granite up over old Bull Creek Road, west of Austin. The hill faced east toward the city. The Hill Grill, a famous Austin watering hole and landmark, before it burned down fifteen years earlier, had perched at the edge of Coyote Hill. A succession of owners had built decks down the hill. All that was left of the Hill Grill were the wooden stairs and decks barely clinging to the side of the cliff. The cause of the fire was never determined and the property had been tied up in litigation ever since, inviting a tangle of investors, banks, mortgage companies, insurance companies, arson investigators, ex-convicts, ex-spouses, disinherited children, executors and administrators; in short, it was a lawyers' paradise.

Wesley considered Coyote Hill his personal refuge. Somehow he obtained a key to the padlock on the gate. Late at night, they drove up the winding road. Donnie opened the gate as quietly as possible, and Wesley drove through; Donnie closed the gate behind them, hopped back in Wesley's car of the year, and then, lights off, they coasted gently down the road, past the burned remains of the restaurant, to the very edge of the cliff. There was no real risk of detection. Despite the *Trespassers Will Be Prosecuted* sign at the gate, the litigants had long since stopped paying for security. But Wesley enjoyed the role of interloper. Donnie decided early on that it was worth all the effort. Sipping beer, they'd look out at the lights of Austin spread out before them.

One night, Wesley handed him another bottle of Coors. "Doesn't it ever bother you that your mother left you and married that Grover guy? Don't get me wrong. Lena's the coolest. Really..."

"Dorrie Louise did what she had to do. Why would it bother me?"

"She left you with a woman who wasn't even a relation. That doesn't bother you? I always knew you were a weird kid." He punched Donnie playfully on the arm.

"I don't think about it." *Not any more.* The first month after Dorrie Louise went away, he cried himself to sleep every night. An eight-year-old boy whose mother had told him she'd see him on weekends. She promised, and most weekends she did come to town, or Lena took him to Grover's rock cottage on Lake Travis. But it was different. He knew she had another life and another family. He told himself he didn't care, and after a while, he believed it.

Dorrie Louise told him she loved him. Lena and Papa said the same thing. He believed them and he told them he loved them too. But he knew not to count on it. He taught himself not to worry about it. By his high school years, he had become the person he was now. He was affable, happy, easy to be with, optimistic, polite and helpful to strangers. If he felt abandoned, he had buried the feeling deep inside. He didn't worry about most things and most people. Everything will turn out all right. *It had, hadn't it?*

Wesley threw his empty beer bottle out the open window and opened another. "Maybe you think that you had it bad, just because you never had a daddy?"

"I don't think that. I have Papa."

"Believe me, there're worse things than not having a daddy, like having one who beat your mama and took a belt to you when you tried to stop him," Wesley explained. "My daddy didn't realize how tough those beatings had made me. But he found out when I was about fifteen. I was a big kid, already a pretty good ball player. The old man came in drunk and started in on Mama. I'd already decided I'd never let him do that again. I beat him to a bloody pulp, the drunken bastard. I ran him off and told him I'd kill him if he ever hit my Mama again, or showed up around there." He took another swig of his beer.

"The thing is, Mama never forgave me for that. She found him unconscious by the road in front of our house. She took him to the emergency room and then she brought him home. That was when I lost any respect for either one of them. So I left home. Coach found me a place to live and I became his star receiver."

They sat in silence. Wesley started the engine with a roar. "Yep. I guess we have a lot in common, you and me. No daddy, or a skunk for a daddy. A mom who left us. Just two amigos out on their own."

There was another reason, besides Wesley being like his older brother, for Donnie to trust Wesley and that was The Deal. One night, after they dropped off their dates, they drove back to Coyote Hill. Donnie didn't remember who the girls were, except that his date had been especially friendly and Donnie was feeling good.

"There it is, D. Ray," Wesley said, "our town, our world, just waiting for the two of us."

Then he described how it would be. "You and me, we're hard-scrabble poor. We took different roads: me, athletics, you, the books. But what a team we are. Together we can do anything we want to. So here's The Deal. I never had a real family and neither did you. You're the closest friend I'll ever have. I'll always have your back and you'll always have mine. So that's Rule One of The Deal, you and me always look out for each other. Right?"

"Right," Donnie agreed happily.

"Because nobody has ever given us anything, and nobody ever will."

Donnie objected, "Lena and Papa have been good to me."

"Sure they have, but you don't know why, and I don't know why.

Coach was good to me too, but I know why. He needed a football player and I was one. There's some reason Lena took you in. Hell, she may not even know why she did it, probably doesn't. Maybe it made her feel good. Maybe she couldn't stand that bastard your mama married. You can be grateful to her for raising you, but that doesn't change one thing."

"What's that?"

"Rule Two."

"Which is?"

"You and me, we have to look after ourselves. No one else is going to do it for us. I don't want them to, anyway. I know what I want."

"What's that, Wes? What is it you want?"

Wesley thought a minute and then laughed. "Shit, I guess I don't really know. But I'll sure know it when I see it. So will you. We'll have to take it when we when see it because nobody else is going to do it for us. Right?"

"I guess so," Donnie said. It sounded awfully serious to Donnie. "Sort of like that Tri-Delt you've been screwing over?"

"I don't kid myself, man. That's the main thing. That's Rule Three of the Deal. You've got to be honest with yourself." Wesley said. "Never pretend that you're doing something for your fellow man. You're doing it for yourself. Never lie to yourself. If we remember that, we'll always be stronger than the other guys, the ones trying to justify what they want to do anyway, and screwing it up, trying to make it fit into some theory of right and wrong and just doing it halfway. Look out for each other, take care of ourselves, and be honest with ourselves. That's The Deal, right?"

Donnie agreed. He wasn't passionate about it, or determined to out-perform everybody, the way Wesley was, but he agreed. He'd never been able to pull off Rule Three as well as Wesley, but he smiled when he watched Wesley do it, over and over, always with success.

After Donnie settled into graduate history work and Wesley became a rising star at Sawbucks Banjo's venture capital fund in Dallas, they were together several times a month. Wesley would either jet in on the firm's company plane, or drive down from Dallas in his new BMW convertible.

He would pick up Donnie at the Haven and they would head for the Warehouse, their favorite bar on West Second Street.

Some weekends, Donnie would borrow Lena's old yellow Cadillac and coax it to Dallas, where he and Wesley explored the night scene along McKinney Avenue. Wesley was well known at Frankie's Sports Bar there, and just as in Austin, there were always girls.

The rest of the time, Wesley was on the road, with frequent trips on the company plane to New York, San Francisco, Houston, or Chicago, chatting up potential investors for Sawbucks Banjo's ventures, big money types who remembered Wesley's great days on the gridiron. Apparently Wesley was very good at what he did.

CHAPTER FIVE

Finishing his free Whole Foods lunch, Donnie's thoughts returned to the article. Wesley had said he wasn't to worry, and he hoped that he was right. It had all been a funny episode to Donnie, at least until today. When the article was published, Donnie got a few phone calls about it from Houston, one from a state senator's office in Dallas, and then the furor was over. Donnie hardly followed the campaign. From the Attorney General's reaction, he guessed that the ads based on his article had turned a landslide for Payne into a very close race, and that Congressman Bob Braeswood had a real chance to become the first Democratic Governor of Texas in two decades.

"I know why I don't like Sam Payne. But why should I like Bob Braeswood? Will he make a good governor?" Donnie had asked Wesley.

"Probably not," Wesley conceded. "He's a plaintiff's lawyer who's gotten rich off the asbestos and tobacco class action cases. At heart he's a labor union guy. He'll try to repeal the Open Shop right to work laws in Texas and change the Workers Compensation system so the lawyers' fees go up. He says he's for a Texas mandatory health care system like Massachusetts. He's for a state income tax. He wants to lower the sales tax and do away with the homestead exemption for people with homes worth more than one million dollars. He wants a higher severance tax on the oil companies."

"Can he do any of that?"

"None of that has a rat's ass chance of getting through the Texas legislature."

"So it's all talk?" Donnie asked.

"It always is."

"Then why Braeswood?" Donnie wondered again.

Wesley paused before replying. "His brother has a car dealership in the Valley. My summer job was there and my rent car came from there. He's my congressman. And look at the alternative."

But Donnie had tried to ignore the election. He was not especially glad to see the reference to his article, even though he was not actually named, in the Braeswood ads. He just about succeeded in not thinking about it, but it had bothered him last night when Wesley proposed several toasts to: "That Great American, the Attorney General" and to "The Hero of San Jacinto," and finally one to: "The Hermit Hero of the West."

Now he could no longer ignore the election, not after the Twin Peaks came calling. Donnie suspected that Payne V did not make idle threats. The adrenal boost he got at the Capitol was wearing off, giving way to a general sense of dread. Not caring was better than this.

I have to go home. I have to tell Lena and Papa, he thought.

He tossed the environmentally friendly coffee cup into the recycle bin and looked one last time at the well-endowed cashier. He smiled. Despite Payne, in some ways he was lucky, remembering last night with The Acrobat. He visualized her athletic body, but then his thoughts turned instead to Cecilia. *Ah, Cecilia,* the bronze-skinned, black-haired Mexican law student with large black eyes, the slender body of a young goddess, and the temper of a jaguar. Cecilia Medina, who was so angry about what he wrote about Santa Anna, that she wouldn't speak to him.

He walked up Lamar to Nineteenth Street and climbed the hill toward the campus. He hadn't seen anyone he could ask for a ride. The blister on his heel was killing him. He turned at the waffle shop and hobbled several blocks west, to the Haven Hotel and home. His thoughts turned again to Payne and his threats to Lena and Papa. The closer he got, the angrier and more worried he became. He hardly noticed the girls strolling back from class on the shaded streets of the West Campus. He didn't even look to see if Cecilia was among them, perhaps returning from a seminar at the law school.

At last he reached the Haven and the same empty parking lot across which he had been dragged earlier in the day. He went into the café. Lena sat at her usual place on the stool behind the cash register. A gold-tipped, slender, filter cigarette drooped from her lower lip. She had on her customary working attire: a waitress's uniform with a large bow on her bony shoulder. She kept her hair dyed bright red, or more to the point, orange, and with her pallid complexion, the orange hair seemed even brighter. She was tall as well as thin, and years of hard work running a residence hotel and a café showed not only in her bony hands and stringy arms, but also in her face. Donnie was surprised how much Lena had aged during the last few years.

She wore a shade of pink for her uniform that clashed nicely with her orange hair and the hot pink walls and yellow floor tile she chose when she updated the café. At the same time, she converted the rooms in the Haven to efficiency apartments, including a two-room apartment for Donnie.

That was ten years ago, just before the enterprise's main source of business, the Daughters of Extreme Charity Hospital, had moved from across the street to a medical complex that was just then rising west of I-35. As far as the Haven was concerned, it might as well have been in another state. The patients' families who used to fill the rooms no longer came, and now the Haven's residents were transients, down market salesmen, and students, mostly of Latino, African or Asian persuasion. The hotel was barely holding on, and Lena would say, "I just hope it makes me a living until I move over there," gesturing with a nicotine stained finger at the Lincoln Washburn Funeral Home across the street, another neighborhood remnant of hospital glory days. In those times, a healthy attitude about death and a realistic estimate of the right level of end-of-life health care, made a funeral home across from a hospital seem logical. At least the funeral home still got business, pretty good business, to judge by the line of hearses lined up in its parking lot, but the Daughters of Extreme Charity's PR staff would never let a funeral home within a ten block vicinity of the new hospital. Death was officially discouraged.

"Oh, thank God, you're back. Where in the world have you been, hon?" she asked. "We've been worried sick."

She handed him a cold Classic Coke in a red can. Irrationally, Donnie wondered why Classic Coke didn't come in a classic Coke bottle.

"Are you all right?"

"I'm fine, Why, were you worried?" He settled onto the stool across the counter from her, trying to decide how to tell her what had happened. His counter space was marked, "No Smoking Area," the only space that was. The customers smoked all over the café, in clear violation of the stringent, politically correct ordinances of the City of Austin. If anyone complained, Lena escorted him to this stool, showed him the sign and blew smoke in his face. Lena did not believe in the dangers of second-hand smoke.

She wiped the counter with a wide circular motion, her ritual. Stowing the cloth under the counter, she said, "Well, according to Cecilia, you were hauled out of here this morning by two men in suits."

"Cecilia?" His heart skipped a beat.

She took another long drag from the cigarette and stared at him. "Yes, Cecilia. She saw you leave in a government car. By the way, you should see more of that girl. I like her. Now tell me what's going on."

"Was Cecilia worried too?" he asked hopefully.

"Of course she was. We all were. Now tell me."

"It's the magazine article. I think the Attorney General may have been a little bit offended." He looked around the café before continuing. The only customer was a small Indian woman wearing a dull colored sari and carrying a thick scent of curry. She sat staring out the window, ignoring them completely. *She doesn't look like a Payne spy.*

"The Attorney General was offended by your magazine article? Now, don't take this personally, honey, but that seems a tad unlikely. He has so much on his mind, stamping out immorality and all."

Donnie didn't know if she was referring to Payne's well known hatred of homosexuals, of whom there were several who roomed at the Haven and who often paid their rent with undecipherable acrylic paintings and possibly obscene sculptures, although it wasn't easy to be sure if they were obscene or not. Or perhaps she meant Payne's theatrical horror at the mention of abortion. Donnie knew for a fact that Lena had provided room and board for more than one young girl through her time at the family planning center down the block. Perhaps it was Payne's claim that he had stopped the flood of Mexican illegals into Texas. Of course, most of Lena's waitresses and maids had never seen a green card and Lena gladly paid them in cash.

Donnie told her about his morning with Sam Eben Payne V. It was his second time through the recital and he punched up the funny parts with the skill of a stand-up comedian. He also tried to downplay the parts he was afraid might be more serious.

While he talked, pausing for her reaction at the laugh lines about Payne hurting his hand or throwing papers, Lena made him a pimento cheese sandwich with a slice of sweet onion and a saucer full of Ruffles potato chips.

She listened closely, as she had all his life. She had provided him the apartment at the end of the hotel's main hall so he would have more independence than he could have in the small owners' quarters behind the registration desk. Donnie's apartment had originally been intended for Papa's study, but he gladly handed it over to Donnie and moved his scholarly pursuits to the small library in the front of the hotel. Papa was Dr. Ralph Rothschild, a retired professor of English at UT, and a poet.

Donnie's apartment included a living room with a couch, TV, a round kitchen table he used for working and eating, a small Pullman kitchen that he never used, except for keeping beer in the refrigerator, a bath and a separate bedroom. None of the other apartments had a separate bedroom.

He did bring girls there. He always followed Wesley's example and saw them home before morning, but not because of Wesley's reason. He didn't want Lena to see girls going in or out of his apartment. He doubted that she would have been surprised or displeased necessarily, but he didn't want her to see, all the same.

All of Donnie's life, Lena had given him a safe place to stay and all the food he could eat, paid for most of his clothes, tuition and books, and made sure he had spending money; more importantly, she had given him love and safety. If he couldn't return her love with as much enthusiasm as he would have liked, that was his fault, not hers. *It's just the way I am.*

Donnie believed that Wesley was wrong and that Lena took care of him because she was a good person who loved him. All Lena asked in return was that he stay in school and "prepare yourself," which she explained over and over again meant that someday not too far off, she would die. When he was a child, he took those warnings very seriously and used to run to her bed every morning to be sure she had not died during the night.

Where would I go if Lena abandoned me too? Even now, he felt dread at the thought of ever losing her, even though he knew that he would, eventually, and that he would not be ready.

Wesley provided a pretty good remedy for those kinds of thoughts, that is, a good party and a pretty girl, not to mention The Deal. Wesley would always be there for him, even when Lena was gone. It had worked all right, at least until now.

It had been Lena's idea that Donnie study history, with the aim of teaching at the college level. Donnie hadn't argued. He knew it pleased her and it didn't much matter to him. History came easily to him, and left him plenty of free time, which he liked. Payne's threat to ban him from teaching would hurt Lena more than Donnie. He dreaded telling her.

Lena took away his empty plate and cleaned the counter. "Oh Hon, it'll all blow over. What can he do to you anyway?"

Donnie took a deep breath. "Well, he's threatening to keep me from getting a job, for one thing."

Lena stubbed out her cigarette stub in her saucer. Before answering, she lit another one. "He can't do that, can he?" She thought a minute.

"What does Wesley say? Have you talked to him about this?" Lena was no more immune to Wesley's charm than any other woman, which was remarkable because Wesley was a football player and her list of favorites didn't include any other football players. She liked Wesley for the same reason everybody else did. He was good-looking, smart and funny, and when he spoke to you, he made you think you were the most important person in the world. Of course, unlike most of Wesley's female friends, she had never had to wait for the call from Wesley that never came.

"He thinks it will be all right."

"Well, there you are then."

"But it's worse than that."

She looked up through the cloud of cigarette smoke. "Worse? How worse?"

Donnie hesitated and breathed deeply. Finally he said, "Payne said, that if I don't swear that my article is a fake, he will make you and Papa pay, that he'll find a way to hurt you. I don't know, maybe I should have done what he wanted. I don't want either of you to get hurt."

"I would never forgive you if you gave in to that bully. Besides, what can he do?"

Donnie shook his head. "I don't know. Plenty, I imagine. He says he can keep me from working. I suppose he could sic the immigration officials or the health department on you. If he's got so much influence at the university, could he hurt Papa some way? I've been imagining all sorts of things." He stared at her, hoping for reassurance.

Finally, she sighed. "I guess we'd better ask Papa what he thinks," referring to her husband by the only name Donnie had ever heard her call him.

For Lena to ask Papa for advice was very bad. Lena only asked Papa's opinion on unsolvable matters, like what to do with the Haven now that the hospital was gone. Sell it to the apartment developers? Convert it to a MacDonald's? What should they do when Bush Junior was elected president? Emigrate?

On practical matters that had a solution, Lena needed no one's advice. Her bank account, her brokerage account, her municipal bond investments with their ladder of maturities stretching out well beyond the time Lena would live to enjoy them, seeing that she was already nearly eighty, all those things she managed with no advice from Papa.

But now she was calling him. "Papa," she shouted out the back door. "Come here, hon. We've got a bit of a problem."

Papa came to the back door, dressed in the green jumpsuit he wore when he was mowing the grass or repairing the doorjambs or touching up the Haven's pink paint. He took off the jumpsuit and peeled the rubber overshoes from his brogues. Underneath the jumpsuit he had a button down Oxford shirt, a rep tie and tweed trousers. He slipped into his corduroy coat with leather patch sleeves, completing his English professor's uniform. Papa was short and stocky, with a full head of gray hair and a well-tended mustache. His eyes were bright blue. When he fired up the pipe Donnie had given him on a birthday, he looked suspiciously like William Faulkner in his Squire of Oxford County days, which Donnie suspected was what Papa intended. He stood erectly when he came into the room and settled easily onto the stool next to Donnie.

"Now," he said. "What's all this? Does it have anything to do with those men pounding on your door this morning?"

After Donnie recounted his adventure still again, Papa shook his head and brushed back his distinguished grey hair with his well-manicured fingers. Lena took good care of his nails.

"Let me reflect on this, Donnie," he said. They waited while he got himself coffee from the big urn behind the counter. Lena looked at him lovingly. Lena and Papa had met when he was an assistant professor of English at the University of Texas and she was a waitress in the Texas Union, taking courses in the extension department at night and on weekends. As unlikely a couple as they were, she had convinced the handsome man that the best way to pursue his career as a poet was to marry her and live at the Haven, which she bought with a small inheritance from an uncle in Colorado.

Papa had written poetry for small journals for fifty years and occasionally there was talk of a volume of his collected works from one of the university presses. Sadly, nothing had ever come of it, except for one small book published by the University of South Carolina Press on the forgotten poems of William Faulkner, which, according to one critic, deserved to be forgotten.

An hour later, they were still sitting at the counter, waiting for Papa's meditation to come to fruition. Donnie had eaten a second sandwich and a piece of chocolate pie.

"Payne didn't kill your appetite," Lena said ruefully, probably thinking of feeding him from now on.

Papa finally came to life. He took out a well-ironed cotton handkerchief and cleaned his glasses carefully. He put them on his Roman nose. "You did the correct thing, Donnie. You stood behind your work and you refused to give into threats. You needn't worry about Lena or me. She's fought off bureaucrats all her life, and I'm a retired professor. I'd like to see him try to do anything to my pension or me. The entire English department would rise up in fury. It would not be a pretty sight."

Donny tried unsuccessfully to picture that. "He seems pretty resourceful, Papa. I just hate that I've got the two of you involved in all this."

His apology was interrupted by the sudden noise of people gathering outside, of cars and vans crowding into the hotel's small parking lot.

"What on earth?" Lena said.

The three of them went to the window and peered out. Rushing to the café entrance were three reporters holding microphones, each trailed by a man with a video camera. They jostled each other, each one trying to get through the door ahead of the others. The first one through was a tanned girl with sparkling white teeth, a shapely body and a low-cut dress. Donnie had admired her on the six o'clock news. The others followed. They thrust their microphones in his face.

"Are you D. R. Cuinn?" White Teeth asked?

He nodded and the red lights on the cameras came on. "What's this all about?" he asked.

She leaned forward, thrusting the mike in Donnie's face. "What do you have to say about Attorney General Payne's statement?"

"What statement?" Donnie tried, unsuccessfully, to tear his eyes away from her bosom.

"This statement," she said, holding it up in front of her.

It was blocking his view, he noted unhappily. "What does it say?"

"Attorney General Payne says that your article about his great-grand-father is a lie and the so-called Sam Houston account is a forgery."

"He was his great-great-grandfather," Donnie corrected her.

She ignored his comment. "Do you deny that you knew that the Payne papers were forged? And that the whole thing is a fabrication of the Braeswood campaign designed to embarrass the Attorney General?"

Donnie searched for a reply, trying to remind himself to be calm.

Before he could think of an answer, Papa came to his rescue. "Mr. Cuinn has not read the statement," he said, inserting himself in front of Donnie and motioning for him to leave. "When he has read it, he will have a reply. Now, step outside, please. This is a place of business."

That's a bit of overstatement, Donnie thought, looking around the empty café. Even the normally imperturbable Indian woman had fled.

Suavely, Papa led the reporters out to the parking lot. *What poetry seminar had taught him how to manage the press?* Donnie wondered. *Has he been secretly preparing all these years for the day he made the Times Best Seller List?*

"Who are you?" someone asked.

"My name is Professor Ralph Rothschild," Donnie heard him say. "I am a friend of Mr. Cuinn. I suggest that before you accuse Mr. Cuinn of anything, you check the State Archives, where you will find complete support for every word that he has written."

Lena drew Donnie into the sitting room behind the registration desk and pushed him into the big recliner. "Sit," she ordered. They waited until Papa had sent the TV reporters on their way.

When he joined them, he had a very grave look, even for Papa.

"Oh, Papa," she began. "You handled that beautifully."

He was silent.

"What's wrong?" she asked.

"Donnie," he said soberly. "This is very bad."

"I know, Papa."

"No, you don't understand. They have checked the Archives, at the Attorney General's suggestion. The State Archivist, some fellow named Drury, says there is no record of the papers ever having been logged into the Archives. He says that it never occurred to him you had planted them, but he admits that it could have happened. To his credit, he did say 'could have.'"

"No," Donnie shouted. "He's lying. Payne got to him!"

CHAPTER SIX

Some hours later, Donnie was still fuming. At six o'clock the three of them sat in front of the television, watching the local news.

"Payne is a devil." Papa puffed intently on his pipe. He sipped a small glass of bourbon, straight. "He must believe he can raise enough doubt about the document's authenticity to discredit it and you, and still win the election."

The news came on. The anchor led with the story: *"Our top story tonight. Questions have been raised by Attorney General Sam Eben Payne about the authenticity of an article in last April's This Texas magazine. The article claimed that Attorney General Payne's ancestor, Captain Sam Payne, was not a true hero or the real captor of Mexican General Santa Anna. Campaign ads based on the article have become a major campaign issue in this year's race for governor. Supporters of rival candidate Congressman Bob Braeswood assert that Attorney General Payne has exaggerated his ancestor's part in the battle for Texas Independence and has concealed that he was sent in disgrace by Sam Houston to exile in West Texas. They have ridiculed the Attorney General's television ads featuring Payne as a Texas hero. According to a statement from the Braeswood camp, 'It was pitiful enough for the Attorney General to run for office based on his ancestor's name. But it really is laughable when it turns out the ancestor was a fraud. Payne has built his entire political career on a lie.' The Braeswood ads depict a drunken Captain Sam Payne, the Attorney General's great-great grandfather, in pursuit of Mexican General Santa Anna. Today's press release is the Attorney General's strongest effort yet to recoup his family's reputation and with it, his own chances for election. The author of the article is D. R. Cuinn of Austin. For more on this story, let's go to our Capitol reporter, Christine Newby."*

The picture changed to the pretty girl who had been outside the café earlier in the day. *"Thank you, Dave. State Librarian and Archivist Jonathan Drury said today that there is no record of the documents ever having been a part of the State Archives. He said Archives security is to keep documents from being removed, not to keep forgeries from being placed there, and that it is possible that the paper was planted. He said that a comprehensive examination is being undertaken to determine if the document is authentic, but that such an examination could take several months, with no answer likely before the election. Meanwhile, the Braeswood ads ridiculing the Attorney General continue to run in major Texas cities."*

"The bastard," Donnie shouted, rising up out of the recliner and shaking his fist at the screen. "He's lying."

Christine Newby was back on the screen. *"Earlier today, I attempted to speak to Mr. Cuinn, at his apartment in the West Campus area."*

The tape fluttered a second and there was Donnie, gazing intently down Christine Newby's dress.

"Oh, for goodness sakes, Donnie," Lena said disgustedly.

He was only on the screen for a few seconds, in all his glory. His features were decent enough. His reddish-brown hair hung down over his forehead. He didn't look like a pipe bomber. But still, there he was, tall, thin, unshaven, faded t-shirt and worn jeans, sandals, typical University of Texas grad student. He looked like a Bosnian refugee. *I wouldn't trust me myself,* Donnie thought.

Christine Newby continued. *"Mr. Cuinn's spokesman, UT professor and author Ralph Rothschild, asserted Mr. Cuinn's innocence."*

The tape rolled again and there was Papa, debonair and in control, telling the reporters to check the Archives, which of course was exactly what they had done.

"Back to you, Dave."

The rest of the evening, Donnie felt he was on a roller coaster from elation to despair and back again. At the peak, he remembered standing up to Payne and made jokes about the day, but at the nadir he worried about Lena and Papa. He half expected a call from his faculty advisor telling him that his application for a teaching fellowship had been rejected, but at least that call did not come.

It was too soon, Papa said. The university had a protocol when pressured by politicians: a call from the politician to the chancellor; a warning by the chancellor to the president to expect a call; a call from the politician's chief of staff to the president sympathizing and expressing regret, but warning of the consequences to the budget process if the politician's request was not acted on; a call from the president's assistant to the faculty dean expressing even more regret. Only after those steps could Donnie expect a letter from the head of the History Department telling him he was not awarded a teaching fellowship, probably because of "budgetary constraints," which in fact would be true.

Wesley called. "Great newscast."

"Do you really think so?" Donnie asked. "I don't see it."

"It shows how worried Payne is. His pollsters will tell him that the more he talks about it, the worse it will be. And tell the professor that he's a natural."

Not long after that conversation, Stu Short, the editor of *This Texas*, called. He spoke in the conspiratorial tone Donnie had enjoyed when Stu was editing the article. It had been fun, a lark. No longer. "The magazine is considering putting out a statement that it has confidence in your research and in your article."

Donnie noticed it was his research and his article. When they were working on it, it was our article. "Considering? Did you say considering?"

"Before we do that, Drayton Philby wants to talk to you." Philby was Stu's boss and the publisher of *This Texas*. Tomorrow morning. O.K.?"

"Sure." Donnie tried not to sound worried.

"Come prepared to tell Drayton exactly what happened."

"I will, Stu. They have it all wrong, really. My article is accurate."

"Well, my ass is on the line. I okayed the article. And Payne's people have gone crazy. They've sworn to turn the Capitol upside down until they prove the whole thing is a hoax. If there's a problem with your research, they'll find it."

"Everything I used was right there, in the Archives. It had to have been there all these years."

"I believe you, Don. I don't have any choice. I have to believe you. Now we need to make sure that Drayton believes you. So you be here in the morning at ten, ready to make that happen, O.K?"

"No problem. No problem at all."

"Until we talk, keep low, don't go on TV anymore."

"What happens next, Stu?"

"The election is still a ways off. The ads have really hurt Payne. That's obvious." He paused. When he spoke, he sounded happy for the first time. "On the bright side, I really do think the article may cost Payne the election."

The election! All this trouble, all for a piece of political propaganda. Was that what the article was, just a campaign ploy? If so, then to that extent, Payne had been right. Donnie didn't feel especially proud.

It was a long, restless night. Donnie must have slept. In the middle of the night, he woke up hungry. As usual, there was nothing to eat in his refrigerator. He stumbled down the hall to raid the café's kitchen. Before he could turn on the light, he heard Lena and Papa talking in the darkened room.

"I'm sick, just sick," Lena said.

"Don't fret, sweet," Papa told her.

"I'm old, Papa. We're both old. I want to see Donnie settled before I die. Is that too much to ask?"

"No. No. It's not too much."

"Do you realize how he depends on us? To me, he's still my little boy. I need to get him settled. Teaching would be perfect for him. I know it would."

"We can't be sure, sweet. This may turn out to be for the best."

Donnie could hear the anger in her voice, anger he rarely heard. "You always say that. What could be 'for the best' about being twenty-eight years old and unemployed and disgraced. What could possibly be for the best?"

"Hush, now," Papa said softly. "I just meant that Donnie might not be cut out to be a scholar. The way he's handling this mess." Papa's voice tailed off and Donnie pictured him shaking his head as he did when he was searching for just the right word. "How hard has he really worked at his studies? He's bright enough, but I'm not sure his heart is in the work."

"You…you…you've always hoped he'd become like you, haven't you? Locked away with his books, protected from the real world? A scholar, like you!" Donnie could hear her scorn.

Papa didn't answer.

"Donnie's not like you. He enjoys life, he loves people, he's funny; he is not like you."

Papa still didn't answer.

"He has to make a living. He may not be the teacher you want him to be, living in an ivory tower, but he has to cope on his own and teaching is a way that he can support himself. He won't have someone to protect him and provide for him all his life."

There was a long silence. Finally Papa said, "I know I haven't been a success. I know you've always provided for me and let me live a cloistered life."

"Oh, Papa," Lena said sadly. "I'm sorry. You know I love you, and I love you just the way you are. You're a poet. You would be a poet whether I was here or not. You had to be. But Donnie is not you." She sobbed. "He's my poor little boy, with no daddy and no mama. Just me. I have to see him settled before I die."

Donnie crept back to his apartment and fell into bed. He tried to remember the good parts of what had happened, but he had trouble recalling any. All he could hear were Lena's sorrowful words.

The sun was high in the sky when he woke up. He had slept at last and he felt refreshed. As he put beans in the coffee press in his small kitchen, he pictured Attorney General Payne in his oversized chair and laughed at the image. He remembered Lena and Papa talking the night before, but decided that Wesley was right. Everything would work out. It always had.

He sipped the strong black coffee and looked around at the muddle that was his apartment. Energized and needing something to do, he decided to straighten his room. This was an urge that came over him about once a month. Most of the time, he let Lupe put things wherever she pleased.

He picked up the clothes that were scattered over his prized black leather couch. It had come from Papa's office in the English Department when he retired. Underneath some shirts and pants he found The Acrobat's silk panties. *Was it only the night-before-last I took those off of her?* It seemed so long ago, so much had happened. He put the panties in a paper bag and stuck the bag in a drawer. No need for Lupe to share yet one more giggle with the other maids about Donnie's visitors.

He showered and dressed carefully. He put on a fresh white Oxford cloth dress shirt, carefully ironed by Lupe, a clean pair of chinos and his leather loafers. He combed his hair carefully, although it quickly fell down over his forehead. He thought a minute and took his one sport coat out of the closet. He did not know what the day would bring, but he was putting that bedraggled grad student behind him. He had a meeting with Drayton Philby and he wanted to look his best.

When he got to the café, Wesley was sitting at the counter, eating a plate of sausage and eggs. He held one of Lena's crisp biscuits lathered with butter in his large hand. Between gulps of food, he was talking with Lena and Papa. Wesley hadn't changed much since he left UT. His hair was a little longer, more carefully groomed. He wore more expensive clothes. He had on a dress shirt made of fine cotton. It was perfectly pressed. He had on a suit of soft gray Italian wool. He had loosened his tie and hung his coat on the back of a stool.

All in all though, it was the same Wesley. He might have been eating Lena's cooking as if he was starving, but otherwise he was obviously satiated. At least it was obvious to Donnie, based on years of observing Wesley after he had all the sex he wanted. There was that look about him.

Lena poured Donnie a cup of coffee. "My, don't you look nice. You look just like a young Robert..."

"Redford," Wesley interrupted.

"Yeah, right," Donnie said.

"What's the occasion?" Wesley asked.

"I've got a ten o'clock meeting with the publisher of *This Texas*." He took a gulp of the coffee. It was strong and had a chicory flavor. He loved Lena's coffee.

"Drayton Philby? Now there's a character. I'll drive you over there. What's the meeting about? Philby want you to write a follow-up, maybe a play-by-play of your meeting with the Attorney General? That ought to be worth a few laughs." He wiped his mouth with a paper napkin and pushed another large forkful of eggs past his glowing white teeth. They had been carefully restored and perfected by an orthodontist who was a UT and Wesley fan, after Wesley's famous game winning goal line collision with Ohio State's star running back Arlon Pheelps at the Fiesta Bowl.

Donnie smiled. "I do not believe he wants another article from me. At least not right now. I think the meeting is where I'm supposed to satisfy him that I'm not a forger or a liar. How do I do that?"

"I don't know, D. Ray. You are resourceful though. Remember that time you impersonated a narc at Patsy's? The place emptied out and we got a table right in front. Cindy loved that."

"Cecilia didn't."

He glanced at Lena, who was shaking her head remorsefully.

"And then there was that time—" Wesley began.

Donnie interrupted him quickly, "Forget the war stories." He nodded toward Lena.

"Lena knows that you're a party animal. She understands that."

"There will be time for jokes when this is all over. Finish your breakfast. I don't want to be late."

Wesley sopped up the last bit of eggs with a piece of biscuit and sighed happily. "Let's do it. But first, I have something for you, Professor Rothschild." He reached into the leather briefcase at his feet. "Have you read this?" He handed Papa a slim volume of poetry from the Oxford Press.

"No, I have not. That's very kind of you." Papa took the book, and without saying goodbye wandered out to the small book-lined alcove. He would probably spend the rest of the day there, reading.

Donnie took one of Lena's biscuits and wrapped it in a napkin.

"Don't think you're going to eat that it my car," Wesley warned.

Lena hugged Donnie. "Mr. All-American, you help my boy get his life back, do you hear?"

Wesley laughed. He pulled Lena into a bear hug. "Lena, I don't care a thing about D. Ray, but I'll never let you down. You can trust me on that." He kissed her on the cheek, holding her close.

She blushed like a girl. "You just mind what I said."

They walked to Wesley's BMW M6 sports coupe. It was new and it was bright metallic red. Wesley waited to unlock the car door until Donnie ate his biscuit and put the paper napkin in the outdoor trashcan. The red Beemer was Wesley's dream car, bought with his first bonus from Sawbucks Banjo. "It cost too much, but I had to have it." He rubbed the sensuously carved fender and smiled happily. "It's smooth, like a woman."

They climbed in. Wesley shifted easily through the gears and drove slowly, but with a BMW roar, to the offices of *This Texas*, just north of the Capitol, and one block from the Attorney General's office. Wesley pulled into the magazine's parking lot. He pulled down the sun visor and examined his teeth in the lighted mirror.

"Nice caps," Donnie said. It was an old joke.

Wesley grinned. "The best tooth man in Texas. I'm happy to give you his name."

"Can't afford him, I'm sure. Besides, my Robert Redford teeth are naturally perfect. And, they're all mine."

They got out of the car. Wesley offered his fist and they bumped fists. "The Deal," they said in unison.

This Texas publisher and generally important person Drayton Philby was well known for the scathing letters he wrote everyone in City and State government, pointing out their ineptitude and general worthlessness. His blistering editorials and rough and tumble journalism were legendary in Texas.

A good-looking young man at the desk smiled winningly at Wesley and directed them to Stu Short's office. The offices at *This Texas* were Spartan; even the managing editor barely had room in his office for a desk and two chairs. Clippings and files were piled as high as his desktop computer.

Stu stood up and shook Donnie's hand. "How're you holding up?"

Wesley answered before Donnie could say anything. "He's doing fine. This is one strong boy. It'd take more than the Attorney General of Texas to frighten Donnie Ray Cuinn."

"Sure," Donnie agreed doubtfully.

"Good." Stu grabbed Donnie's arm and steered him into the hall. "Drayton wants to see you right away. Just remember. Every word you wrote is well-researched and fully documented. Got it?"

Donnie nodded. *Of course I've got it. It's the truth. What does he think I'm going to say? That I faked it?*

The publisher's office was as luxurious as the other offices were plain. It wasn't as large as the Attorney General's, but almost. It had two separate conversation areas with leather chairs and glass top tables. There were antique bookcases along the walls, filled with leather bound volumes. An English partners' desk was centered on a room-sized Oriental rug. Framed cartoons from Nineteenth Century editions of *Punch* covered an Oriental screen. Cover art from apparently memorable issues of *This Texas* were framed and hanging on a wall. Two men were seated across from each other at the desk. A younger man stood behind them.

One of the men, who Donnie took to be Drayton Philby, stood when they entered. He had a florid complexion, was somewhat overweight, and wore a black patch over one eye. The young man was quickly at his side. He guided Philby by the arm. Donnie hadn't known that the famous publisher was blind.

The unpatched eye stared ahead and up a little, not quite on the mark when he turned his head toward Donnie. His full head of dark hair was carefully combed and had recently been razor cut. He was tieless and wore a blue patterned dress shirt open at the neck under a dark blazer with expensive looking gold buttons engraved with the initials "D.P." He fiddled a little with his shirt collar and Donnie could see that his nails were buffed and manicured.

"Come in, my boy," the blind man said. "It's good to see you." He laughed as he said it. Waving back at the other man, he said, "Do you know Sid Banger?"

An emaciated looking man with a bad complexion, thinning hair and round rimless glasses in a rumpled suit, peered up at Donnie. Slowly, he extended his hand. "Pleased to meet you, Professor."

Was he being sarcastic? Probably, Donnie thought.

"Sid is a political consultant with the Braeswood campaign," Philby explained.

This meant nothing to Donnie, who had not read any of the dozens of articles that credited Sid Banger with Braeswood's surprisingly success-ful race for Governor.

"Come sit beside me, Don. I want to know our prize historian better. Let's sit by the window, Geoff."

The young aide guided Philby to a leather chair in front of the large window that overlooked a small garden. Water rushed into a koi pond and Donnie could make out the shapes of the orange and white fish darting back and forth just under the surface of the water. Geoff motioned for Donnie to take the chair next to Philby. Banger, Stu and Wesley seated themselves in a semi-circle facing the publisher. If Wesley hadn't been in-vited to the meeting, he acted as if he had. That of course was Wesley.

"Damn nuisance being blind," Philby said, settling his large frame into the chair. "Yes, a damn nuisance. You'd think I could find my way around my own office. I've been working here for more years than your age." He looked toward Donnie and smiled. "What are you, under thirty?"

"Twenty-eight, Mr. Philby."

"Drayton. Call me Drayton." He paused for a minute. "No matter how many times I tell them not to move anything, the cleaning crew de-lights in moving my furniture around, just to see if I'll fall and break my neck." He smiled tightly.

Geoff, the aide, protested. "Now, Drayton." He spoke softly. "It's the turnover. We always tell them, whenever there's a new cleaning person."

"No, no, it's impossible, really. They refuse to understand how dev-astating moving something a few inches can be to me. Fortunately, I'm lucky enough to have assistants, like Geoff here, around the clock, really, ready to lay out my clothes, get my coffee, drive me anywhere I need to go. They do anything my poor heart desires. And they never complain." He patted Geoff on the arm. "Well, hardly ever. They live in my house, three at a time. University students. Geoff here is Plan II. He wants to be a journalist, don't you Geoff? Listen and learn. It's valuable clinical training you're getting here. I should charge you instead of paying your exorbitant stipend."

They all chuckled. Donnie observed that Geoff's smile seemed a little strained.

Stu cleared his throat. "Drayton, Donnie had an exciting meeting yesterday with our friend the Attorney General."

"Yes, yes, of course. I know the man. He's an idiot. All this ruckus about the article just makes his situation worse." He reached over and gripped Donnie's arm tightly. His grip was very strong. "But we'll get him. You'll see. If not this time, then the next election. Eventually we'll get him. I'm hopeful it will be this time."

He removed his hand from Donnie's arm. "I'm very determined. And so is my magazine. Just ask Wendland Turner."

Donnie raised his eyebrows.

"Former Speaker of the Texas House of Representatives," Stu explained to Donnie.

"Former, is correct," Philby said. "Everyone knew he took pay-offs from that Amarillo bank. Of course, they said it could never be proved, and if it was, that an Amarillo grand jury would never indict, and if they did, that an Amarillo jury would never convict. Well, it took eight years and three trials, but Turner is still in prison in Huntsville. We hammered and hammered and...." He slapped his hands together. "Finally, we got him." He looked around. "Coffee, Geoff," he ordered. "Where are your manners?"

Geoff sprang to his feet and hurried out the door.

They sat quietly, waiting for him to return. "Do you know why I am so determined, my boy?"

"No, sir."

"Because of this." Philby pointed to his eyes. "Stu and Sid know, but you may not, that I was blinded in a car wreck when I was fourteen. My older brother was driving." He paused. "Dealing with my blindness taught me never to give up. I had to struggle every day, but I was determined to do all the things everyone else in school could do. It was the same in college, and it's the same with the magazine."

"I think that's amazing, sir. I really do."

"Of course it didn't hurt that my father was one of the richest men in Texas, owned three hundred thousand acres of timber in East Texas." He laughed. "Or that he never forgave my poor brother for that accident and left everything to me. So I can run this magazine how I please, not kowtow to any politician or any advertiser. And you know what? *This Texas* makes money, lots of money."

Donnie wanted to ask what happened to the older brother, but decided against it.

Geoff returned, pushing a coffee cart, followed by a Hispanic boy wearing black pants and a long-sleeve black shirt. When he placed a cup in front of Philby, the blind man patted the boy gently on the butt.

Oh, Donnie thought. He looked at Wesley and raised his eyebrows. *What was that all about?*

Wesley winked.

They settled back, sipping coffee. It wasn't as good as Lena's. Philby moved his cup toward the table. Quickly, Geoff guided his hand to the correct spot. "Thank you, Geoff." He turned again to Donnie. "So tell me about D. R. Cuinn and his adventures at the State Archives. Tell me exactly how you discovered the infamous document."

The group listened silently while Donnie told his story: how he had spent months working on his thesis about Sam Houston and anti-bellum Texas; how he was working in the Archives, finishing up his research, when he came across the paper, wrapped in oilcloth and stuck in the back of one of Houston's old ledgers.

"It was an indescribable feeling, touching something that Sam Houston himself placed there. It probably hadn't been disturbed since he put it there."

"They actually let you touch it?" Philby asked. "It must be fragile."

"It was. No, you have to wear these thin cotton gloves when you handle anything at the Archives. When I saw what it was, I asked for a copy to be made. It was a week before I finally got a copy I could really examine. I spent that time reading about Captain Payne. I didn't think the week would ever pass, I was so excited." Donnie knew he was pouring it on a little thick, but he sensed that thick was what Drayton Philby wanted to hear, and Wesley nodded encouragement as Donnie told his story. Truth be told, he hadn't been quite that excited. His main thought was: *Maybe this will be a good finish to my damn thesis. I'm ready to be done with it.*

"I understand exactly what you're saying," Philby said. "What a remarkable discovery."

"That's it, really. I'm sure you already know how Stu offered me the chance to write the article for *This Texas*."

"Yes, yes. So tell me about your meeting with the Attorney General."

Donnie recited in detail his meeting with Payne the day before. He told about Payne banging his fist and throwing papers and the terrified notary public in the corner of the room.

Philby let out a big belly laugh. "What an ass-hole. All that bluster and you didn't give an inch." He clapped his hands together. "Good for you, my boy! Good for you!" He stared hard at a spot above Donnie's head. "Now I have to ask you the most important question of all. Do you know what it is?"

"I imagine I do, sir." Donnie shifted a little in his chair.

"Yes. You probably do. You realize that my magazine's integrity is the most important thing in the world to me. More important than anything," he repeated. "That is what gives us the moral high ground when we go after a scoundrel, one like Payne, for example. Of course, Payne is one of the better examples of scoundrel, even for *This Texas*." He raised his empty coffee cup in the general direction of Geoff, who took it from him with a well-practiced flourish.. "So I'm going to ask you this vital question." He paused dramatically. "Do you have any reason to believe that the document is not genuine?"

Donnie answered immediately. "No, none whatsoever."

"Have you any reason to suspect such a thing?"

"No, sir." Donnie was emphatic. "Until yesterday, such a thing never occurred to me. It happened just as I've told you."

Philby stared toward Donnie for long seconds. "He'll come hard after us and after you," he warned. "He'll use every weapon the State provides him, plus some that it doesn't. Do you understand that? Are you ready for that?"

"Absolutely. I hate him."

Sid Banger spoke for the first time in his slow Southern drawl. "Good job, Professor. Let's send the Attorney General back to West Texas with his tail between his legs, just like Sam Houston did his granddaddy."

The others laughed cheerfully. Philby and Donnie shook hands.

"We'll do our part." Philby searched for Donnie's knee again. He found it and gave it an uncomfortably long pat.

Donnie glanced at Geoff, who didn't look pleased.

Donnie's cell phone rang. He apologized, then looked at the caller I.D. "It's Lena." He looked questioningly at Wesley.

"You'd better take it. Lena's his step-mother," Wesley explained to the others.

Donnie went out to the hall. Lena spoke slowly; Papa said that the more excited she was, the slower she talked. "Your friend has struck again."

"Payne? What did the bastard do now?"

"After you left, two men who said they were from the Attorney General's office came here, looking for you. They said they had some more questions. Also, they said they wanted into your apartment. They said they wanted to examine your computer and your files."

"They can't do that. You didn't let them in, did you?"

"They had badges, but we took care of those Fascist pigs, hon."

"Took care of them how, exactly?"

"Cecilia did it. She came as soon as I called her."

Cecilia Medina, the Mexican girl never far from Donnie's thoughts, was an attorney. She was working on her doctor of laws degree at the University of Texas Law School. Donnie's thoughts about her had never involved the law, at least not until now.

"Cecilia demanded to see their warrant and of course they didn't have one," Lena continued. "She asked if this was a criminal matter and they finally admitted it was not, so she told them to go away. They threatened to come back with some sort of subpoena. Cecilia says she doesn't know what they will do next, but she suspects Payne has the entire Attorney General's office working on your case. She thinks they'll get some kind of order to force you to turn over your files and testify."

She stopped for breath, and then sighed. "Donnie, if this place had a reputation, you'd be ruining it."

"That's wonderful."

"Be serious, Donnie." He heard her strike a match and light a cigarette.

"No, I mean, it's wonderful that Cecilia is helping. I didn't expect that. She hated the article so much."

Lena chuckled. "She hates Payne more than she hates you."

"Oh, well then. That's a comfort. Tell Cecilia I'll be home right away."

He hurried back to Philby's office and recounted his conversation.

Sid Banger spoke up in his nasal twang. "The last thing we want is for you to give a deposition right now, or for your notes to be taken out of context and splashed across the morning papers. Payne's looking to smear you."

Philby stood up. "I suggest you collect your things and leave town right away. Don't tell us where. If Payne's talking litigation, he'll sue us too. He'll probably claim we libeled him. Don't worry. We've fought libel lawsuits many times."

Donnie shook his head. "Why should I run away? I didn't do anything wrong."

Banger growled. "Listen, Professor—"

Before he could finish, Philby cut him off. "Don, you need to listen to our advice. I know you want to fight. And you will. But for now, do what we ask. It's for the best. Please."

Donnie looked to Wesley, who nodded agreement.

"We'll get the bastard, but on our own terms. For now, you need to be out of sight," Philby reiterated.

Donnie sighed. It didn't seem right. "I know a place I could go."

"Dorrie Louise's?" Wesley whispered.

Donnie nodded at the mention of his mother.

Stu broke in. "Get your computer and your files and get out of Austin. We can defend ourselves, but you'll probably need your own lawyer."

"I think I've got a really good one." Donnie smiled.

"Good!" Philby said. "Now go!"

CHAPTER SEVEN

Lena, Papa and Cecilia were standing guard in Donnie's apartment when he and Wesley walked in. Donnie held out his arms to Cecilia. "Thank you for being here."

She hugged him. "I'm still angry with you." She gave her long hair a toss. Her black eyes flashed. "But you're harmless, I suppose. Payne is a menace."

Wesley laughed. "That puts you in your place, D. Ray."

"Well, thank you, I guess." Donnie smiled at to Cecilia. "Payne doesn't seem to think I'm harmless."

Cecilia shook her head impatiently, "We need to make some plans. We need to get you out of here, until we find out what Payne is going to do."

"I'm thinking about going out to Smithberg and staying with Dorrie Louise for a few days. But I really hate to run away, especially when Payne's threatening Lena and Papa. What do you think?"

Cecilia did not hesitate. "I think you should go, right away, before the A.G.'s people come back. Go out there and let me handle the legal side of this. I'll look after Lena and Professor Rothschild."

"Cecilia," he began.

"Just go. This isn't about you. It's about a power hungry Attorney General."

"Do you hate him that much?"

"Well, let's see. He wants to arrest all illegal immigrants and make them serve time in tent prisons in the desert before they're forcibly deported; he wants to arm vigilantes and give them permits to shoot people

73

crossing the border; he wants to do away with English as Second Language training in Texas schools; he wants to end health care for Mexican nationals in Texas; he wants to ban Mexican trucks from Texas highways; he wants to keep Mexican-Americans from voting in Texas elections; and according to you, his ancestor tried to rape a Mexican hero. Plus, he will do anything to win this election. Other than that, I have nothing against him."

His opponents are pretty good at that last part too, Donnie thought, but he kept the thought to himself. He knew he was looking at Cecilia like a grateful puppy, but he didn't care. He was that happy to have her on his side.

"Lena, can I borrow the Caddy?"

Before Lena could answer, Wesley interrupted. "No offense, Lena, but that old heap should have been junked ten years ago." He gritted his teeth, the sign he was making a hard decision. He handed Donnie his keys. "Here. Take my car."

"The Beemer? Are you sure? I might get some crumbs inside it."

"I'm sure. Now let's get you out of here."

They grabbed Donnie's files and computer from his apartment and loaded them into the small trunk of Wesley's car. Donnie went back to the apartment and took a quick look around. He hated to be chased out of his home, as humble as it was.

Cecilia stood at the door, watching. "Hurry, Donnie. Don't worry. I'll take care of everything here."

Nodding gratefully, he stuffed a change of clothes and his toilet gear in his old duffle. They rushed to the parking lot. He threw his duffle in the backseat, next to Wesley's Tumi suitcase.

"Careful you don't scratch the leather. You have no idea how much that suitcase cost."

Donnie hugged Papa and Lena. He held his arms out to Cecilia. She gave him a half-hug, then said, "Sigue! Rápido!"

He smiled and said, *"Me alegra que estés de mi lado."*

"It's not about being on your side. It's about Payne. Que bastardo. Now go. *Ahora sigue.*"

While they packed the car, they agreed that Donnie would drop Wesley at the airport, where the Banjo Sawbucks' company plane was waiting. Then Donnie would drive to Smithberg.

Wesley insisted on driving to the airport. "If I don't see it happening, maybe I won't think about you driving my car."

He drove past the entrance to the International Airport, so-called because of its one flight a day to Mexico City, to the general aviation hanger. A gleaming white Lear Jet was waiting on the tarmac.

"Well, Crud." Wesley cuffed Donnie lightly on the back of his head, "Try to stay out of trouble for a change. Look on the bright side."

"There's a bright side?"

"Yes there is a bright side," Wesley laughed. "There definitely is a bright side. You just can't see it yet."

Donnie shook his head. "I'm running away. That can't be right, can it? I shouldn't be leaving Lena and Papa alone."

Wesley hauled his bag out of the back seat and handed it to the company pilot. He turned to Donnie. "They're not alone. Let Stu and Philby and that snake Sid Banger handle Payne."

"And Cecilia. Don't forget Cecilia."

"Who could forget Cecilia? You just stay out of sight."

They shook hands, did a little shoulder patting, said "The Deal" softly to each other. Wesley loped across the tarmac, bounded up the stairs and ducked into the cabin of the Lear jet.

Donnie turned the BMW around and left the airport. Two miles from the airport, he took a right turn onto Highway 183 for the drive to Smithberg. He stopped in the parking lot of the Cowboy Boot and Western Wear Store, and fiddled with the BMW's confusing German controls. At last he got the top down and the radio on. He pulled quickly into traffic; he pressed hard on the accelerator and felt the engine respond with a sharp lunge, pressing his head back against the leather headrest. He was on his way, accompanied by *Tristan* on Classical Radio 89.5.

Twenty miles north of Austin on Highway 183, he came to the turn-off for Smithberg, the small community where Donnie's mother, Dorrie Louise, lived with her husband Grover Smith. Donnie took the left turn and headed down the winding two-lane road that skirted the lake. He drove through the green canyons and under the ancient cedar trees that drooped over the road, taking his time, enjoying driving the BMW.

When Donnie first started coming to the lake alone, not having to wait for Lena to drive him out, or for Dorrie Louise to come to town for him, he took the bus to Cedar Creek and then walked eight miles down the country road to Smithberg. That was fifteen years ago, and now the city had spread out this way, near but not quite to, the village of Smithberg itself. Almost every tract of land directly on the lake was subdivided, and metal roofs and limestone walls reflected in the sunlight through the cedar trees.

A mile or two back from the lake, the old brush country was still there, although even there, some of the scrub cedar trees had been cleared and building sites hacked out of the hard tack caliche, leaving vacant sores ready to be filled by trailer houses or double-wide manufactured homes.

It wasn't until he got to Smithberg itself that he felt out of the sprawl, and that was because the land was too rough, the roads were too bad, there were no utilities, and the lake itself was too far away.

Donnie had called Dorrie Louise on his cell to tell her he was coming, but it wasn't necessary to call. She was always at work. She and Grover ran the country store in the little town named after Grover's grandfather. Dorrie Louise was there all day, every day, tending the cash register, stocking the shelves, and selling beer and soft drinks to the boaters and fishermen who came through on their way to the remote fishing holes further up the lake. If the cook was too hung over to come to work, Dorrie Louise took over for him in the kitchen, cooking breakfast or frying hamburgers.

Grover spent most of the day in his real estate office, a cluttered space he had carved out of a corner of the store. Maps and plats and scribbled plans to subdivide more pieces of the land he had inherited from his father covered his old oak desk. The Smith land was worthless except for a small piece that Grover called "lake view." That is to say, if you climbed the tallest tree on the property you might catch a glimpse of the lake. *On a clear day*.

Grover's fondest hope was that the government would take his land for an endangered wildlife preserve, paying him an inflated price and saving him the problem of trying to sell it off, a quarter-acre lot at a time. He claimed that his property was a nesting ground for black-capped vireos, the endangered birds that resembled underfed starlings left for dead in the Sahara. The government had set aside an obscene amount of money to buy "habitat" for these ugly birds, and Grover desperately wanted as much of the government's money as he could get.

Donnie suspected that Grover was lying about the sightings of vireos on his land. His photos and affidavits seemed about as trustworthy as Roswell UFO photographs, but Donnie was prejudiced. He believed Grover was a low-life horse's ass, who had married Donnie's mother when she was young and with no husband to protect her and no father for her young son. Grover had worked her like a galley slave ever since.

Donnie disliked Grover Smith the first time he met him and the years hadn't changed his opinion. Donnie was six when his mother first brought Grover to the Haven Hotel. The stocky man smelled strongly of cigar smoke.

Grover put his hand under Donnie's chin and lifted his head up. "Look at people when they say hello, little buddy."

Donnie ran to his mother and put his head in her apron.

"Shy little booger, ain't he?" Grover patted Donnie on the head awkwardly. "Needs a man around, I guess. No Daddy and all."

The meeting between Lena and Grover did not go well. Donnie supposed many conversations were lumped together in his consciousness, probably amplified over the years by snatches of later remarks between the three adults in his life, Dorrie Louise, Lena and Papa. Wherever they came from, the memories were still there.

"He wants to marry me, Lena. What should I do?" Donnie looked outside. The strange man sat in a beat-up pickup truck, the window rolled down and the cigar smoke swirling in the afternoon heat.

Donnie looked up at the two women. "Go play, little hon," Lena told him. "Your mama and I need to talk."

Donnie looked at Dorrie Louise, who leaned down and gave him a kiss. She pushed him off. "Go in the back and find Papa," she said gently.

Donnie left but he did not go outside. He sat on the floor outside the door of Lena's office and listened to the women talk.

"Why would you marry that man, Dorrie Louise? You can't love him?"

"He's not a bad man. He promises he'll take care of me and Donnie, and he'll move Daddy to a better place, out near Smithberg." Her daddy, Donnie's grandfather, was in a nursing home in south Austin. Every Sunday afternoon they visited the old man, who sat silently in a wheel chair, not speaking and giving no sign he recognized his daughter or her son. "It's terrible where he is, but it's all we can afford, just whatever his Social Security will pay for."

"You take on too much, Dorrie Louise. That man kicked you out when you were pregnant with Donnie and now you're giving up any chance of happiness so he can be in a better nursing home?" Lena's skepticism was warranted. The old man died not long after the wedding, before Grover had to pay to relocated him. *Lucky bastard.*

"I'm his only daughter, Lena. But it's not just that. I need a husband. Donnie Ray needs a father."

"Hmmph," Lena snorted. "Remember when you came here, carrying that baby in your arms? I told you then that there was a place for you both here. There always will be. You don't have to do this. I've never understood why you never told Donnie's real father that he had a son in Austin."

"He never knew about the baby."

Donnie's real father, as best Donnie could reconstruct, was in the National Guard and had been called to fight in one of the foreign wars the country was always messing around in, and Dorrie Louise had been too ashamed to tell him she was pregnant. When he came back, he went home to Denton and married his childhood sweetheart, without ever knowing about his son in Austin. Donnie had driven to Denton with Wesley once, looking for the man listed as his father on his birth certificate, but when he found the nice brick house Marvin Cuinn was living in, and saw the swing in the side yard and the basketball goal over the garage door, he had lost his nerve.

"Leave the man alone," Wesley had advised. "Nothing good will come of it," and Donnie had agreed.

Dorrie Louise was determined to marry Grover, whatever Lena said. The little boy didn't know what it all meant, but he shrank from his mother's new friend. After weeks of whispered conversations, Lena made her final proposal. "Leave the boy with me. The schools out there are awful. Leave him with me," she pleaded.

Of course Dorrie Louise refused but Lena told her, "Just watch Grover with him. If you think he'll be a good father to someone else's little boy, then you're blinder than I thought."

She finally wore Dorrie Louise down. She admitted at last that Donnie would be better off in Austin. She came to him and tried to explain. "We'll be together on the weekends. You'll go to a good school here. Lena will take good care of you."

All Donnie heard was that his mother was leaving him, to go off with the cigar-smoking man. He cried and begged her not to do it, but Grover pulled her away and they were gone. So Grover got Dorrie Louise, without the senile grandfather or the illegitimate son. The *lucky bastard*, he thought again. Dorrie Louise could have left him and come back, and for several months Donnie thought that she would, but it never happened.

"Some women just have to have a husband," Lena said to Papa. "It doesn't matter how worthless he is, as long as he wears pants."

Lena tried to comfort him, but it was no use. He cried day and night every time Dorrie Louise left.

"Take me with you," he would beg, and his mother would look tearfully at Lena and at her new husband.

"It's better for him here," Lena said, and of course Grover agreed.

After they left, Lena said, "You don't want Grover to be your daddy, do you? Papa and I will look after you from now on, I promise."

"I just want my Mama," Donnie cried.

It took months, tears and fearful goodbyes every weekend, but one day he just stopped crying. When he saw Dorrie Louise, he would smile and let her kiss him. He learned not to think about her. Lena gave him anything he asked for and Papa read him poems and stories, and over time acting happy turned into being happy. *None of that other stuff mattered.* He did well at school. His classmates liked him. He didn't have to try very hard to get good grades.

"You need to find something to be passionate about," Papa urged.

Donnie smiled and agreed, but he didn't change. Passion had gone out of his life when his mother left. Passion was dangerous. He woke up each morning, not worrying what was going to happen, knowing he would have a good time.

So it was that he was Donnie Ray Cuinn, son of Dorrie Louise Smith, but reared by Mr. and Mrs. Ralph Rothschild. No wonder the Attorney General's goons had trouble deciphering his family background. Donnie had trouble deciphering it himself.

It was all too complicated for Grover's simple mind. To him Donnie would always be Dorrie Louise's bastard. Grover hadn't wanted Donnie then, and he had never acted glad to see him during the boy's weekend or summer or holiday visits. As he got older, Donnie assumed that Grover's indifference, make that belligerence, was because he feared that Donnie intended to lay some kind of claim to his "estate," which was how he referred to the one thousand acres of land located four ravines back from Lake Travis, and that Donnie might end up with part of the fortune he expected to leave to Donnie's three half-sisters.

Donnie pulled up in front of the store and whistled a little sigh of relief when he saw that Grover's pickup truck wasn't there. He went inside. The familiar smell of barbequed brisket filled the room. His mother was alone, sitting at the counter. She looked up from her Globe Magazine.

"Hello, Donnie Ray," she said with a little smile, pushing her graying hair back from her eyes. He hugged her. The pretty, slender girl who had married Grover was still visible despite her tired eyes and aging face. The hard life keeping the store and raising three daughters *and, God knows, living with Grover,* had taken its toll—she wasn't even fifty.

Lena said Donnie looked a lot like Dorrie Louise, the same rusty hair and blue eyes and fair complexion that ran to freckles. She said he got his height and skinny frame from his real daddy. "I hear that he was a string-bean too," she said. "But you get your dimples and your disposition from your mother. I just hope there's not a female Grover out there somewhere, waiting to latch on to you."

Dorrie Louise put down her magazine. "Let me fix you a sandwich."

Donnie murmured a polite refusal but knew it was useless to argue. It was one thing she could do for him.

"You need to eat. Look how skinny you are." She went around the counter and through the door to the kitchen. "You need to eat."

They were alone in the store. He stood at the open kitchen door and watched her standing at the old butcher block counter beside the black oven and griddle, both spotless despite the thousands of burgers and strips of bacon that had been cooked there. They talked while she made him a thick brisket sandwich.

"How are the girls?"

"Just fine." A little light came into her tired eyes when she talked about Donnie's half-sisters. "Betty Ann got that job in Houston, the one I told you about? She's got a cute fellow who's after her to get married, but she's told him she's not ready."

"Good for Betty Ann." It was hard for Donnie to imagine that his little half-sister was already out of college, working as a high school counselor.

"She says she wants three years to get established in the school system. Then she'll think about getting married."

"Good for her," he repeated.

The other two girls were both in college in San Marcos, one a senior and one a freshman. All three made good grades. All three were on a path toward meaningful work and a sane life. Somehow, all three girls had escaped Grover's bad genes—no doubt thanks to Dorrie Louise, and were turning out well.

He sat with his mother at the counter, eating his sandwich. The wooden bar was shiny and worn and also very, very clean. He decided his mother took out her frustrations on the appliances and counter tops. He took a bite of the sandwich. The thick slab of brisket was tender and flavorful from the long time it had been on Grover's wood smoker behind the store.

In between bites, Donnie told her a little about his run-in with the Attorney General. "I really made him mad. He's threatening to keep me from getting a teaching job."

"He's such a handsome man," she said, referring to Donnie's archenemy. "I can't believe he would threaten you. Did you know his grandfather was the Hero of San Jacinto?"

"It was his great-great-grandfather, Dorrie Louise. I truly believe that if he'd been there, Sam Eben Payne would have thrown the Battle of San Jacinto."

"Oh, Donnie Ray," she giggled. "You shouldn't talk like that."

Donnie could see the girl when she laughed. She must have been beautiful. *No wonder Grover had wanted her, even with a bastard son,* Donnie thought.

He tried to explain the details of his situation, but she shook her head. "I don't care about all that, Donnie Ray. Just tell me what I can do to help you. Do you need money?"

"No, no," he assured her. "I just need a place to stay for a few days. Is the cabin empty?" He was referring to the hunter's cabin that Grover rented out during deer season. Grover owned a half dozen cabins up by the road, but Donnie was talking about the one set back in the cedar trees, the one where Donnie had spent his summers.

"Of course it is. You can stay back there as long as you want to."

"Will Grover mind?" He knew the answer. Of course Grover would mind. "I'd rather not have to explain to him why I'm hiding out."

"Oh, Donnie Ray, that's silly. You're not hiding out. You're visiting your Mama. And she's really glad to see you." She reached for him and he embraced the small woman in his arms and she kissed him on the cheek. "And that's all Grover or anyone else needs to know."

There was a squeal of tires on gravel outside. Donnie looked up in time to see Grover Smith park his lime green pickup truck next to the BMW. He climbed out, squinting at the convertible, his potbelly stretching his cotton plaid shirt over the top of his starched jeans. His over-sized cowboy hat had settled down on his balding head, framing his big ears and tufts of already gray hair. He came inside, slamming the screen door and looking unhappily at Donnie.

"Fancy ride for an unemployed college boy."

Donnie thought about explaining the car was Wesley's. He decided not to bother. *If it worries Grover, so much the better.*

Grover stared at him. "Git me a beer, Dorrie Louise." He settled his overweight frame onto a stool at the counter. He looked at Donnie with obvious distaste.

"Hello, Grover," Donnie said, taking the last bite from his sandwich. He imagined, with pleasure, that Grover was calculating how much the brisket had cost him.

"Donnie Ray's going to stay in the cabin for a few days." His mother smiled pleasantly.

"Not if somebody wants to rent it, he's not." Grover took a long swig of his beer. "To what do we owe this honor?"

Dorrie Louise answered quickly. "He's going to spend a few days with me before he goes to work. He has a job at the University of New Mexico, don't you, Donnie Ray?"

"Uh, that's right," Donnie lied. "Albuquerque. I start next month." Lying to Grover was no sin, he was sure of that.

Grover brightened considerably at the news that Donnie was moving six hundred miles away. They stared silently at each other for a few minutes.

"Some good news on the Endangered Species Preserve, Dorrie Louise," he said at last.

"What's that, Grover? Did the Commission meet?"

"No, not yet. Next month. And Smithberg is first on the agenda. I've got to get my bird pictures enlarged and my affidavits ready. The staff says there's a real good chance the Commission will approve it. If they do, they'll take the whole place. At my asking price. Imagine that."

Donnie could not imagine that. *Surely any sane person, or even any State employee, can tell Grover's bird pictures are fakes.*

"It all depends on the Chairman of the Commission. If he says yes, we're home free."

Donnie was afraid he knew the answer, but he asked the question anyway. "Who is the chairman?"

"Why, Attorney General Payne. He's the Chairman of the Endangered Species Commission."

Donnie smiled. He got up and said he would like to unpack his things.

His mother gave him the key to the cabin. "Come back for supper. We can watch *Wheel of Fortune* and visit."

He turned to Grover. "You don't have a thing to worry about. I was in the Attorney General's office just yesterday."

Grover looked at him with suspicion. "You? Why?"

"Oh, some political business. You know, University of Texas stuff. I met with General Payne personally. Just him and me. And two of his trusted assistants."

"That so?" Donnie could almost hear the few wheels in Grover's undersized brain beginning to turn.

"That's right. So just tell Payne that you're married to my mother and stand aside and watch things happen."

"Damn, boy," he said, shaking Donnie's hand, "that's a hell of a idea. Goddammit, I'll tell him you're my son! You really met with him in his office? Yesterday?"

"I certainly did, Grover. And I can assure you of one thing. He knows who I am."

Donnie smiled at Dorrie Louise, who giggled and waved when Donnie went to the car. He sat in the BMW for a few minutes, relishing the picture of Payne ripping Grover's bird pictures to shreds. He might even get indicted for perjury, with all those fake affidavits. *Surely Dorrie Louise will tell him the truth. But will she?* He couldn't be sure. Finally, he went back into the store.

Grover looked up expectantly. The Prodigal Son returned so soon!

Donnie spoke softly. "Grover, you better not mention me to Payne."

"Why not?" He looked up suspiciously.

"Well, the thing is, he hates my guts. He's blackballing me at every state university. That's why I'm moving to, uh, New Mexico, to get as far away from him as I can. If you'd get cable out here, watch the news or read the Austin paper, you'd already know about it."

As Donnie left, he heard Grover say to Dorrie Louise, "Don't tell me any more about it. I don't want to know!"

CHAPTER EIGHT

Donnie unpacked his things from the BMW. He settled into the familiar cabin easily. Nothing much had changed since he was there last. A comfortable double bed stood in one corner with a good reading light beside it. A sink, a small refrigerator and microwave were in the opposite corner, along with a round table and two wooden chairs. On the wall opposite the door was a fireplace made from local orange rocks. There was a small bath with a sink, toilet and shower. Altogether, it was everything a person could want, Donnie thought.

He felt tired. He went outside. One summer he had bought a hammock and strung it between two large oak trees. It was still there. He needed a nap. He climbed into the hammock and fell asleep almost at once. He didn't wake up for two hours.

Over the next few days, he settled into a routine, eating his meals at the café with Dorrie Louise, ignored by and ignoring Grover.

The ring of his cell phone startled him at about 8:00 a.m. on the fourth morning. It was Cecilia.

"Well, hello. Do you miss me?"

She ignored him. "We need to talk."

"What's wrong?"

"A couple of things. The INS showed up yesterday to check everybody's green card. Fortunately, Lupe saw them coming and they didn't catch anyone. While they were here, the City Health Department inspectors drove up, to check the kitchen for health violations."

"Payne's work, do you think?"

"Of course." She sounded impatient with him. "What do you think?"

"Maybe with no workers we won't need the kitchen."

She sighed. "Can't you be serious for once? Anyway, the only violation Health found was an open tuna can in the kitchen."

"I'll bet that fried Lena. Whose fault was that?"

Cecilia laughed. "Hers. Apparently she was making Papa some tuna salad when the inspectors got here."

It was good to hear Cecilia laugh for a change. "Will they be back?"

"Who knows? Lena can handle those guys. There's something else we need to talk about."

"You want me to come back?"

"No, no. That won't work. I'd better come out there."

Donnie tried not to show his excitement at the thought of being alone with her at the cabin. "Well, all right, if you need to. Do you know the way?"

"I believe I can find it. I'll leave in a few minutes."

Donnie turned to cleaning up the cabin and making the bed. He called Dorrie Louise and told her to send Cecilia to the cabin when she arrived.

He sat on the porch, trying to read, but unable to think about anything except the slender, dark-eyed Mexican girl with a face like an angel and an unforgiving nature. They had dated a few times, to the movies or for a cup of coffee; they had ridden their bikes on the bike trails, out Shoal Creek Road and back through Northwest Hills; they had walked in the park down the hill from the hotel. They had run the jogging trails around Town Lake. She seemed to enjoy his jokes and stories. He avoided stories about Wesley.

He offered to cook dinner for her at his apartment and she came, bringing a bottle of Malbec from the winery of an Argentine friend of her family. They talked about school, about History Department gossip and what the law school was really like. It had been fun.

After dinner one evening, they sat on the black leather couch. He poured her another glass of wine. "Tell me your story."

"My story? What do you mean?"

"I want to know about you. You're a mystery woman, from an exotic land far away. Tell me about yourself." He reached over and brushed her hair back from her eyes.

"Where shall I begin?"

"At the beginning." Donnie reached for her hair again. She pushed his hand away.

"Well, to begin at the beginning, I am Mexican."

"I never would have guessed." Donnie smiled.

She told him about growing up on her family's ranch in Guerrero, not far from Taxco; she told him about being tutored at home until she was old enough to go to convent school in Taxco; she told him about her love for horses, about learning to ride. She told him about taking a lunch and riding for hours, all the way to the foothills that led to the mountains twenty miles from the family ranch. She told him of the beauty of the land and the people.

"You must miss it."

"I do miss it. I missed it when I was in Mexico City at the university and law school, but at least I could get back every few months. Here, it's a world away."

"It's not so far, is it?"

She thought a minute. "Not so far in kilometers, but it's a world away in every other way."

"Why law school?"

"Well," she said with a little pride, "I'm good at it, and the family needs a lawyer who understands Yanqui law. My father is developing land outside

Acapulco with my uncle, my mother's brother. They have American investors. My own brother is in the import-export business, making money in NAFTA, the North American Free Trade Agreement."

"Is that what NAFTA stands for? I never knew," Donnie confessed.

"Poor little history major. Knows so much and yet so little."

"Ouch."

"It made sense for me to come to El Norte and study commercial law. That way the family won't have to hire expensive Houston lawyers to do its business. Besides, I already have an offer from a law firm in Mexico."

He took her wine glass, put it on the floor and reached over and kissed her.

After a second, she pulled away. "No," she said. "I don't think so."

"Why? You know how much I like you."

She stood up and went to the door, looking back at him sitting on the couch. "I like you too, Donnie. But I don't want to have a relationship with you." That was the only explanation she gave him.

He didn't give up and they continued doing things together. He hoped that with time, things would be different. He thought about her a lot, even when he was with The Acrobat. Then the article was published and things were different, but not in the way he had hoped.

Cecilia was fiercely protective of her Mexican heritage and she made no secret that she thought Donnie's article defamed the Mexican President. "Your article is insulting to General Santa Anna. You make him out to be a womanizer, a coward and a fool," she said angrily.

"Which one wasn't he?" Donnie joked. That was a mistake.

"You are impossible to talk to. Everything is a joke to you."

"That's not funny," Donnie replied with a grin.

"You see? You even joke about joking. Do you want to know why I do not want a relationship with you? You're just a wanna-be fraternity boy. All you like to do is drink and screw around. You're not serious about your work. If I wanted a fraternity boy, I've had plenty of opportunities. But I'm a grown woman, and I want more than that in a man. The idea that you could write that article and not even think about its effect on people, well, that tells me even more about you." After that, she had not spoken to him until the Attorney General's goons tried to raid his apartment.

Donnie hadn't expected that result. In fact, he had not even thought about Cecilia being Mexican when he wrote the article, and for that he had no one but himself to blame. The article was just a lark. *Why did she have to take it so personally? And it wasn't fair to call me a frat boy. I have a master's degree, for God's sake.* He had to admit that he and Wesley partied a lot and he enjoyed it. *But that doesn't make me a bad person.*

Stung by her words and aching for her, he turned to his expert for advice. He asked Wesley what he should do. Wesley didn't hesitate to tell him.

"Tell her what she wants. Agree with her. Admit you're a bastard. Promise to change. That's all it will take. She's ready to hop into bed with you; all she needs is an excuse. Give her one."

"And when she finds out I lied to her?"

Wesley sighed. "D. Ray, we've had this conversation before. Who's the one person you don't want to lie to?"

"I know, I know."

"Well, who? Say it."

"Yourself. Don't ever lie to yourself."

"Right. It's part of The Deal. It's no different with Sawbucks' investors. I don't believe all the bullshit I tell them. I know I'm giving them a snow job. In their hearts, they know it too. The important thing is the payoff. If they make money, they're happy; if they don't, they're pissed. It's the same with women. It's the same with everything in life. Just be sure you know exactly what you're doing. Don't ever lie to yourself."

"But what if I love her?"

"Love her? Haven't you learned anything, all the times we've had together? You tell yourself you love her, when really all you want is to fuck her. Tell yourself the truth. You can tell her you love her, if you need to, to get in her *calzones,* but don't fool yourself."

"You really are a crud, Wesley."

"That's high praise, D. Ray. Let me tell you. There's two kinds of women. One kind is like Cindy: no illusions, no games. She likes me, she wants to screw, she understands. The other kind is like your Latina. She wants to screw too, but she needs to be romanced, she needs to be lied to. I can handle both kinds. In fact, I like the variety."

"And when the second kind finds out you're a liar?"

Wesley laughed. "She likes it. She likes that I took the trouble to lie; she likes what I give her; if she needs to, she convinces herself I'm lying about the lying, that I really love her, or maybe I'll change. Proof is, I've never had a woman leave me. It's always me who leaves."

Donnie shook his head. "Cecilia is different."

Wesley chuckled. "No, she's not. She just needs a good fucking. I could have her in bed in a week, if I wanted to."

"You stay away from her," Donnie said. "I mean it."

"Sure, sure," Wesley said. "But she is *una dulce chica*."

Donnie heard the sound of Cecilia's Yaris stop in front of the cabin. He went to the screen door and smiled at her.

She didn't smile back. This is all business, her look said.

"Come on in," he said, holding the screen door open.

Instead, she sat down in one of the chairs on the porch. "This will do." She was wearing a pair of shorts and a sleeveless top, and carrying a leather briefcase and a small thermos.

"Can I get you a drink?" he asked hopefully. He sat down in the porch swing and tried not to stare at her long legs.

"I have tea." She lifted her thermos.

"So what's up?" Donnie rocked slowly back and forth in the swing.

She took some papers out of her briefcase. "Do you know who State Senator North Tompkins is?"

"I think so. Isn't he from up around Dallas, somewhere?"

"Right. A rich suburban district, big Payne district. Tompkins is chairman of the Government Facilities Oversight Committee in the State Senate."

"Good for him."

Cecilia looked at him impatiently. "But maybe not so good for you. His committee has responsibility for the State Archives." She handed him a document.

"Subpoena? What's this?"

"Tompkins has called a special meeting of his committee." She took the subpoena from him and read, *"To investigate whether fraudulent documents were introduced into the State Archives and to consider possible referrals for criminal prosecution."*

Donnie smiled, but a little more tightly now. "They're going to force me to testify?"

"You figured that out all by yourself? That's what the subpoena is for."

"All I can tell them is the truth."

Cecilia shook her head. "Don't you see? They'll have the State Librarian…"

"Drury?"

"Yes, Drury. They'll have him say that there's no record of the Payne document in the Archives, and so, it must have been planted. One of you has to be lying. If they believe him, you could go to jail."

"Well, they'll just have to believe me. Let's go back to town and I'll testify."

Cecilia put down the papers. "As your lawyer, I can't let you do that. It's too risky."

Donnie smiled. "You're really my lawyer?"

"Of course I am. Aren't I?"

"Why?"

"Why what?"

"Why do you care?"

She put the papers back in her briefcase. "I told you before, this isn't about you. It's about Payne and his attitude toward Latinos. It's about Lena and Professor Rothschild and keeping them from being hurt. It's about your mother. I want to protect her if I can."

"But it's about me, a little bit, isn't it? Admit it?" He reached over and took her hand in his.

She drew her hand back. "You're hopeless."

He leaned forward in the swing and tried to put on his best earnest face. "Cecilia, I've been thinking about what you've said. I have been selfish. The Payne stuff was just an interesting footnote to my thesis. I should never have written the article. I'm sorry that I did. I apologize if I hurt you, or anyone else."

She stared at him a long time, then she said, "Tu estas lleno de, Donnie. Absolutely full of it."

Donnie gave her his *aw shucks* grin. It usually worked, but not this time. "Well, it was worth a try."

With a flick of her hand, she said, "Get me a beer and let's figure out what we're going to do about Senator Tompkins and his committee hearing."

They sat on the porch until sunset, trying to decide what to do. Donnie reviewed his visits to the Archives and Cecilia made detailed notes.

"I must have been down there a half dozen times, and I never saw Drury."

"And when was it that you found the Payne paper?"

"Like I said, it was the last time."

"Tell me exactly what happened."

He thought before continuing. "I had been looking at Houston papers, his diaries and some letters."

"And was that when you found the Payne document in the back of the journal?"

"I'd been there a few days, looking at different source materials." He paused. "I remember that a clerk brought me this journal. He brought it and he said 'Here's the last of the Houston material,' or something like that. I hadn't seen it before, so I thumbed through it carefully. You know the documents are all protected with plastic. But this was stuck in the back of the journal. It was wrapped in oilcloth. It looked like it hadn't been touched in a hundred years. I said, 'What's this?'"

"What did the clerk say?"

"Nothing. He just shrugged and left me alone."

"But he saw you take the paper out of the back of the journal?"

"Absolutely. He saw me and I asked him, 'What's this?' and he shrugged and walked away."

Cecilia looked at him, excited now. "Well, there's your defense. What was his name?"

Donnie shook his head. "I have no idea."

"Think, Donnie. Think."

Donnie grimaced. "I have no idea."

"What did he look like?"

"A nerdy looking bald guy, glasses, I don't know. He had on a nametag, I remember, with his first name on it, and I called him that. He'd retrieved books for me before. He's the same guy who told me I had been banned from the Archives the other day. But I can't remember his name."

She stood up. "Do you get the Internet out here?"

"Believe it or not, I do." He pointed inside. "My laptop's in there, on the table."

She went inside. He stood over her as she clicked through web pages and called up the personnel directory for the Archives. "There. That's the employee list. Don Addams, Jim Bedrich, Clay Costin..."

"Wait." He leaned down, looking at the screen. "That's it. Clay. His name was Clay."

"Good. Let's just look through here and be sure he's the only Clay." He was. She put her papers away and stood up.

"What next?"

"Next, I'm going to see Mr. Clay Costin and get him to verify your story."

"Use your feminine wiles on him?" Donnie joked.

"My smile is like a sword unto me," she answered as she started to her car.

"Thank you, Cecilia. I mean it." He smiled. "Are you sure you won't spend the night?" He gestured toward the cabin.

"Perfectly sure, Mr. Cuinn." She opened her car door and sat down. "Please stay out of sight if a process server shows up." She started the engine and drove away.

Donnie sat alone on the porch, listening to an owl and watching the stars. To the east, he could see the night-lights of the city. Ten years ago, Austin was too far away to be seen. Now it was just over those hills. Then he hadn't worried about what was going on there. Now his thoughts were with a dark-haired girl in a little Yaris on the road into town, helping him and his family because she believed it was the right thing to do. He sat for a while longer, then went into the cabin.

His laptop was still on the kitchen table. He sat down and opened up Google and typed in "General Santa Anna."

CHAPTER NINE

A day passed with no word from Cecilia. But early the following morning, she called from her car. "I'll be there in twenty minutes. Pack your things," she ordered. "Clay Costin is in Mirabeau. We're going out there. Get the BMW ready."

He packed hurriedly and told Dorrie Louise he was leaving. He had just put some of Dorrie Louise's doughnuts in a paper bag, when he heard Cecilia's car screeching to a halt in front of the cabin.

She tossed her overnight bag in the back seat of the M6. "I want to drive," she demanded.

"Please do not tell Wesley," he said with a shudder. But he gave her the keys."

They left in the coolness of the early morning, going west on US 290, with the sun rising behind them. He had put the top down on the BMW and they had to scream to be heard above the wind.

She handled the V10 engine like she had been driving sports cars all her life, running through the seven gears easily and reaching ninety miles per hour in a heartbeat. She looked at him with a smile. "My God, I'm good."

"So tell me what happened." Donnie leaned against the car door so he could look at her. The scarf she had tied around her head had blown loose and her hair was free in the wind.

She looked over at him quickly and then back at the road, steering the BMW effortlessly on a steep hill, around a thirty-eight foot Fleetwood RV and ducking in front of it just in time to avoid a gravel truck in the opposite lane. "It seems that your friend Clay Costin is gay," she shouted.

"I did not know that, but thinking back, I'm not surprised."

"Why, did he put a move on you?"

"Who could blame him? I'm irresistible."

"Well, he definitely is gay. He's with his partner at their place in Mirabeau. His partner is an artist and has a studio out there."

Mirabeau was a small town about five hours west of Austin.

"How did you find that out?"

She smiled and slowed down to eighty. The noise subsided. "From a co-worker. Who isn't gay? I think he likes me."

"Of course," Donnie said. "I hope you didn't do anything you'll be sorry for."

"No, I didn't do anything. What he thinks or hopes I might do, now that's another matter. But when I explained to him in my cute little Spanish accent, that I was a girl who just had to find Mr. Costin before Monday, and how eternally grateful I would be, he gave me Costin's cell phone number and volunteered that Clay spends a lot of time in Mirabeau with his partner."

"That was nice of him." Donnie handed her a doughnut. She bit into it and he watched her brush the sugar off her chin.

"He also couldn't wait to tell me about Clay's sexual orientation. He made it pretty clear that he thinks the Archives gives preferential treatment to gays and lesbians."

"Talk about your reverse discrimination. Maybe that's why he was so eager to help and not your irresistible beauty."

She flashed a grin at him. *"Imposible."*

"I just hope your charms work as well on Costin. Maybe you can do a Barbra Streisand imitation."

"People, people who need people, are the luckiest people in the world," she sang.

They stopped for gas and a cup of coffee in Johnson City. The coffee shop was tucked in behind the gas station. The place was empty except for a group of ranchers at a round table in the rear. He held up two fingers to the waitress and mouthed "black." In a minute, she brought them two cups and a pot of coffee that she set on the table.

"We've got some great blueberry pancakes, folks." They shook their heads and she wandered to the back of the café, trading jokes with the men.

They sipped their coffee quietly. Donnie took a breath and said, "You were wrong about Santa Anna, you know?"

She looked at him sharply. "What do you mean?"

"For one thing, he was no saint."

"I never said he was. I said you were unfair to him."

"He was dictator three times. He lied to everybody. He was cruel and he killed his enemies. He'd go into exile and lie and cheat his way back into power and then kill the people who befriended him. He sold the United States the Gadsden tract, for God's sake." He paused and poured them both some more coffee.

"That should make him a hero in your eyes, the Gadsden Purchase. What did that do, fill out land you forgot to steal in 1846 after you took *La Mesilla?*"

"Santa Anna wanted the $15 million. We wanted the land to the Rio Grande."

She shook her head angrily.

He went on. "But you were right about one thing."

"What is that?"

"I didn't even look it up. I didn't try to make the article balanced. I didn't try to find out anything about the Mexican perception of what happened. That's more important than whether Santa Anna was a whore-mongering scumbag of a dictator, which he was, by the way."

She smiled. "Good of you to put it that way."

"No, really. You were right, are right. Why was it that the Mexican people took Santa Anna to their hearts so many times? They knew what he was, but they did it anyway. I can't ignore that question, not if I want to make any sense of what happened."

She shifted her weight on the wooden seat. "And you want to make sense of it, is that what you're saying?"

"I think I do."

They sat in silence. "Why?" she asked finally.

He squirmed a little in the seat, stretching his legs under the booth, careful not to touch hers. "Maybe Payne has done me a favor."

"Really?"

"Yes. I was so angry with him, it was like someone turned a switch on."

"What does that mean?"

"It's hard to describe. All I know is, some things are important to me now, things I would have laughed off before."

"What things?"

He thought for a second. "Well, Lena and Papa of course. I can't let that bastard hurt them, not if I can stop him. Then there's my work. For the first time, I guess it matters whether it's right."

"Fair and balanced?" She smiled softly. "Like Fox news?"

"No. Just that I get it right."

"That is important."

"Then there's you."

Their eyes met. "Me?"

"Yes. I want to get that right too."

She stood up. "I think we need to get you out of this mess. Let's go."

Mirabeau was a small town that lay in the foothills of the Davis Mountains. Named after Mirabeau B Lamar, the second president of the Republic of Texas, it was founded after the Civil War by ranching families that owned most of that part of West Texas. The ranchers' wives needed a place to gather, exchange gossip, shop and teach their daughters about civilized society. The wives' ferocious determination to bring some form of culture to Mirabeau had spawned reading clubs and art guilds and music societies. It had attracted piano teachers, music directors, bookstores, and from time to time, whole colonies of artists. Writers, painters and artists of all stripes still came there to work and enjoy the cool climate and tolerant society.

In the 1970s and 1980s, wealthy professionals and independent oilmen seeking to escape Houston, had built weekend homes in the Hill Country around Austin. However, the area developed so fast that whatever it was they were seeking became difficult to find in Austin. Austin was dangerously close to becoming the new Houston.

A few pioneering Houstonians discovered Mirabeau, and in only a few years, the same shops and café and people that the Houstonians were escaping, began to spring up in Mirabeau. Mirabeau became the new Hill Country. The ranchers and the artists, in an unlikely coalition, hated the newcomers.

So did the survivalists, a large number of whom had settled in the remote area, where they hoped to escape the end of civilization, which they believed was rapidly approaching. They joined forces against the newcomers—the ranchers by overcharging them for scrub land without water; the artists by mocking the Houstonians' artistic pretensions and overcharging them for the most mediocre works in their galleries; and the survivalists, who saved most of their petty crimes and brutish confrontations for the arrivistes.

There were still parts of the original Mirabeau remaining, although their owners prospered mainly by selling their quaintness to tourists. The Mirabeau Pharmacy and the Hotel Osso were two examples.

Cecilia finally slowed down when they got to Mirabeau's Main Street. "Over there," Donnie said, pointing across the street. "That's the world famous Mirabeau Pharmacy."

She made a quick U-turn and pulled into a space in front of the wooden building. It was decorated with rusty ranch tools. There was a landing on the second floor with wooden banisters like the ones in old Western movies that cowboys fell through after they were shot. The sign above the landing read *Original Mirabeau Pharmacy.*

They went through the screen door and found themselves in a 1940's drugstore. A long soda fountain and counter ran down one side of the store. Signs advertizing milk shakes and banana splits were tacked between the large mirrors behind the counter. Wooden chairs and tables filled the center of the room surrounded by counters and shelves filled with candy, souvenirs and camping gear.

Several families, apparently tourists, judging from the maps and guidebooks they carried, sat at the tables, their overweight bodies overflowing the wooden chairs. They were attacking big bowls of ice cream.

Wooden columns, which reached up to an old tin ceiling, were covered with survivalist posters announcing meetings and end-of-the-world supplies. Donnie pointed the signs out to Cecilia. "I read that Mirabeau is the home of the Republic Militia."

"What in the world is the Republic Militia?" She sat down at a vacated table and looked around the room.

"It's a group that's been attacking organized government in Texas for ten or twenty years. They believe the world as we know it is coming to an end. They've declared their independence from Texas and the U.S. They want their own state out here, so they can survive Armageddon."

"Sort of like the Texians did in 1836."

"If you say so."

A shaggy-haired man sat on a stool behind the soda fountain, reading a newspaper. Cecilia got up and went to the counter. "Excuse me. Do you know a man named Clay Costin?"

He shook his head. "No." He pointed to a telephone book on the counter and went back to his newspaper.

She looked through the telephone book. "He's not listed. I'll just call him on his cell."

"Milk shake?" Donnie asked.

"Hmm, chocolate." She thumbed briskly through her briefcase and proudly held up a sheet of paper. "His number."

Donnie watched her, admiring the excitement in her eyes. He ordered two chocolate milk shakes. The shaggy haired man sighed, put down his paper and turned to making the shakes.

Cecilia talked rapidly on her cell. She had finished by the time the milk shakes were ready. Donnie took them back to their table.

She put a straw in the thick drink and sipped hungrily. "Mmm, so good." She wiped her lips. "He agreed to see us, once I told him it was you."

"He remembers me?"

"It sounds like you made a real impression on Mr. Costin. Just turn on your charm when we get there."

"Promise you won't be jealous?"

"I promise."

When they finished their shakes Celia said, "It's about thirty minutes from here. He gave me directions. His partner's name is Adalgar Widmark.

"Who's that?" Donnie asked.

"Adalgar Widmark...the Sculptor."

"I'm supposed to know who that is?" Donnie went to the cash register to pay. "How about Adalgar Widmark? Do you know him?" he asked the shaggy-haired man.

"Everybody knows Adalgar. Are you going up there?"

"Yes. He's a sculptor, right?"

"So they say," the man answered. "So they say."

"But you don't think so?" Donnie picked up his change from the counter.

"Sir, I'm not a critic. If people from Dallas and Houston want to buy that stuff, then good for Adalgar." He turned the page of his newspaper. "There may be something about Adalgar's place on that table over there."

Donnie looked through the literature on the table. There were notices about art galleries, poetry recitals, a flute recital. Sure enough, partially hidden by the others, was a flyer for the "Sculpture Studio."

It was a good thing the flyer had a map to Adalgar's studio, or they would never have found it. They drove north out of the town, past the restored nineteenth century fort, straight out of a John Wayne movie, complete with its green parade grounds, and then past the Observatory.

A few miles farther, they came to a gravel road on the right, marked by a large sign on which "Sculpture Studio" was spelled out with round red reflectors. They turned onto the road and began a winding ascent, first through some shaded meadows where a few cows grazed, then on to a hilltop that was bare except for an airplane hanger a mile or so distant.

Cecilia stopped the car. "That must be the studio." She drove cautiously over a cattle guard into a fenced pasture, and onto an even bumpier, more winding gravel road. They passed a large sign. *Studio Ahead Visitors Welcome.*

At the first turn, Donnie was startled by a sculpture; at least he hoped it was a sculpture, of a giant metal insect mounted on a concrete base. It was at least ten feet tall and appeared to have been made entirely out of automobile hubcaps. At the next turn was another mammoth sculpture, this made of anodized iron. It was a series of large inverted Vs, hanging from an iron rod. On its top was a cowboy hat made out of aluminum, at least that's how it looked to Donne. The rest of the pasture was filled with more of what he assumed to be Adalgar's work, all exhibiting extreme cases of gigantism.

"Lovely," Donnie said.

"*Filisteo.*"

"I know what that means."

They finally got to the hanger. A two and one half ton army cargo truck was parked in front of it. A large seal was on the door of the truck.

Donnie pointed at the seal. "That looks official. Republic Militia."

"Oh, great," she replied. She parked the BMW next to the truck.

Six men dressed in army fatigues were sitting under a grape arbor attached to one side of the hanger. They watched them but did not speak.

Donnie waved at them and called out, "We're looking for Clay Costin. He's expecting us."

One of the men motioned to the door. "You need to speak to Adalgar, in there."

Cecilia and Donnie went through the door into an alcove. It was dark and windowless. Beyond the alcove they could hear the sound of an air compressor. Following the sound, they entered a large workshop. There, standing over a piece of metal, wearing a welder's mask and holding an MIG welder, was a large man dressed in coveralls and a protective vest.

When he saw them, he shut off the welder, cranked down the valve on the gas tank and flipped up his mask. "Goede middag." His Dutch accent was brusque.

Cecilia approached the man, extending her hand. "I'm Cecilia Medina. You must be Adalgar Widmark."

The man nodded, shaking her hand.

"I spoke to Clay Costin on the phone. Is he here?"

"What about?" Adalgar said. "Clay is busy, very busy, getting ready for our show next weekend. Are you interested in my work?"

Cecilia smiled. "I'm very impressed by it. We both are." She motioned at Donnie who took her cue and shook his head in agreement. "But we need to talk to Mr. Costin about a matter relating to the Archives."

"Clay works for the Archives." Adalgar had a thick accent, cobbled over with a Texas drawl. It was unsettling. "In Austin, he works for the Archives. Here he works on our show. See him in Austin about the Archives." He returned to his welding equipment and began to open the valve on the gas tank.

Donnie stepped between the man and the large piece of metal he was welding. "We need to see him. It's very important."

The big man sighed impatiently. "Go. Go now."

"Not until we see Clay," Donnie insisted. "He knows me. I'm a friend of his. This is very important."

Adalgar set his helmet on the bench and looked closely at Donnie. "What is your name?"

"Don Cuinn. We met at the Archives."

"Clay never mentioned a friend of that name. I know all of Clay's friends. Clay would not have a friend that I do not know. Now go."

Donnie shook his head. "Not until we see Clay. Where is he?"

"Did you see the men outside? If you will not leave I will have to call them. They will be happy to be sure you leave."

"You mean the Republic Militia? I thought they were all in jail."

Adalgar brushed past Donnie and started toward the door.

Cecilia touched Donnie's arm. "We'd better do what he says, Donnie."

"No." Donnie was unwilling to give up.

Just then, a slender figure with a shaved head appeared in the opposite doorway. He wore a tight tank top, cut-off jeans and sandals. It was Clay.

"Adalgar, what's going on?" His question ended with a shrill accent on the "on." Then he saw Donnie and Cecilia. "Don!" he screamed. "It's really you, way out here in the hinterland! Adalgar, you remember I told you about the good-looking grad student who was doing research on Sam Houston? I was right, wasn't I? Isn't he divine?"

Adalgar glared at Clay, then at Don. *If looks could kill, Donnie thought, although not very originally, I would already be dead.*

The big man shook his head. "We're busy. We have to get ready for the show."

"Oh, the show. The show isn't for two weeks," Clay said breezily. "I'll get the blast e-mail out today, don't you worry your cute little Dutch head about that. Just go on with your welding for the Aryan Nation or whatever they call themselves."

"The Republic Militia." Adalgar's tone softened a little. "I've told you before, they're not white supremacists; they're survivalists."

"Whatever." Clay held out his hand to Cecilia. "You must be the charming lady I talked to on the phone."

Cecilia shook his hand. "I'm Cecilia." She smiled when Clay put his arms around Donnie and hugged him.

With a quick glance at the big Dutchman, Clay finally turned Donnie free. "I can't believe you came all this way. Come in, come in. Espresso?"

He winked at Cecilia and whispered. "I just love to make Adalgar jealous." Adalgar had donned his welding mask and returned to his welding.

"Does this mean I'm not divine?" Donnie asked.

"Oh, no, darling, you are, and I suspect Miss Cecilia agrees. Too bad."

Donnie had to shout to be heard over the sound of the welding equipment. "Is there some place we can talk?"

Clay nodded his head. "In the gallery." He led them out of the work-room, through a dark curtain, and into an immense gallery half the length of the airplane hanger. Several colossal, incomprehensible metal sculptures were placed around the room. Skylights had been cut in the hanger roof and daylight streamed down on the sculptures. At the far end of the room was a desk with a computer. Clay pulled up chairs made of welded chains and motioned for them to sit down. He sat behind the desk in a chair covered with yellow fabric.

"Don't you love what we've done with this old hanger? It was Senator Forman's you know. He kept a helicopter here and he used the bedroom upstairs to meet his girl friends. The family ranch is right over there." Clay made an extravagant gesture in a generally western direction. "After he died, the widow couldn't wait to get rid of the place, and that's when we bought it. A perfect studio for Adalgar and a perfect retreat for me, far from the stresses of the State Archives."

"Your work is very stressful?" Cecilia's tone was sympathetic.

"Dear, you cannot imagine."

Donnie spoke up. "You and Adalgar seem quite close to the fellows outside."

"It isn't exactly a natural fit, is it? A gay Dutch weightlifter turned metal-working sculptor and the Republic Militia." Clay giggled. "You'd be surprised how incompetent survivalists are. Heavens, I'm more mechanically inclined than they are. Adalgar is quite clever, really, as well as being the most *avant-garde* sculptor in the greater Mirabeau metropolitan area. It sells like crazy, you know. His work is on lawns all over River Oaks and we just shipped out his latest work to a buyer in Highland Park.

"Anyway, Adalgar says, we don't want those fellows mad at us, which they would be inclined to be, considering their level of intelligence and natural hostility toward same sex couples. So Adalgar has become the Republic Militia's Official Welder. He's putting some kind of armor plating on that truck of theirs. All for free. It's cheap protection, he says."

"Surely you don't agree with their politics?" Cecilia asked.

"God, no. But they like Adalgar so much that they've convinced themselves that we aren't gay. Isn't that a hoot?" He rummaged around on his desk and pulled out a copy of *This Texas.* "So, down to business." He poured them each a small cup of espresso. "Your article has caused quite a stir. Quite a stir. Rumor at the office has it that my boss is livid."

"That would be Jonathan Drury?" Cecilia asked.

"Yes. Well." He smiled coquettishly. "He isn't my direct boss or anything like that. I'm just a poor underling several layers of management below the powerful Mr. Drury."

Cecilia sipped the espresso. "This is wonderful."

Clay started to explain his brewing techniques but Donnie interrupted him impatiently. "You know Drury has told the press that I planted the Payne paper in the Archives."

"Oh yes, I saw that. Just because no one has ever noticed it before, and because it doesn't have a catalogue number. Well, I could show Mr. Payne dozens of items in the Archives just like that. It's absurd."

"He seems pretty positive." Donnie put down his cup.

"Of course he would. He's never worked a day with the documents. He's not an archivist. He's a librarian. He was head of the Dallas Public Library before Senator Tompkins got him this job."

"He and Senator Tompkins are friends?" Donnie asked.

"I don't know if they're friends or not, but Drury is married to Tompkins' first wife's sister. Whether they are still friends, now that Tompkins has left his wife and married his legislative assistant, I don't know. I do know that Drury owes his job to the Senator."

"Ooops," Donnie said.

Cecilia spoke up. "We're here because Tompkins has called a committee hearing on Friday about whether Donnie planted the paper in the Archives. He and Drury will testify."

Clay sighed. "Drury will probably say whatever Senator Tompkins wants him to say."

"And that will be whatever the Attorney General wants him to say," Cecilia added.

"I'm afraid so." Clay jumped up to brew another round of coffee.

"You do remember, don't you, Clay?" Donnie asked. "When I found the paper in the back of Houston's journal? You saw it in there, didn't you, before I ever touched it?"

Clay threw his hands up dramatically. "Of course I remember. It was so exciting. I'll never forget it."

"Would you appear before the committee and repeat what you just told us?"

Clay flounced imperiously. "Of course I will." He refilled their espresso cups with the dark coffee.

"It will make Drury very unhappy, I imagine," Cecilia warned.

"You think?" Clay smirked. "Perfect. Shall I print out a statement for you?"

"Clay, that would be so helpful," Cecilia said. "And Donnie would be more grateful than you can imagine, won't you, Donnie?" She nudged Donnie with her elbow.

"More than you can imagine," Donnie said, wondering what that might involve.

They sat at the desk, watching Clay type furiously. He finished with a flourish and printed out a copy. "Do you approve?"

They read it over quickly. It was exactly what he had told them. "We do," they said in unison.

Clay signed the statement. "I could have the Secretary of State of the Republic Militia witness this, if you want. He's right outside."

Donnie led Cecilia through the lobby of the Hotel Osso and into the Wrangler's Club, the only place in Mirabeau where a celebrating couple could get a drink. They sat by themselves at a table on the balcony, at eye level with the head of a giant antlered buck. They were laughing and joking about Clay and the consternation he would cause Drury and Tompkins when he showed up in Austin for the hearing.

They drank tequila and talked. Then they had another and sipped it quietly. Donnie looked intently at her. "I meant it, you know."

"Si`?"

"What I said at the coffee shop, on the way out here. I meant it. About getting it right. With you."

"I believe you." She touched his cheek with her hand.

He was flushed and her hand felt cool. He was flushed from the tequila, but also from being here, so close to her.

"You're coming out from under Wesley's domination."

"Is that it?" He took her hand in his. "Maybe I'm trading his domination for yours." He kissed the palm of her hand.

"That's entirely different." She smiled and kissed his hand in turn.

"Te gustaría ir a la cama conmigo?" he asked in a whisper.

"Mucho."

Hurriedly he found the desk clerk and arranged for a room. He went back in the bar. She was waiting for him with a quiet smile on her face. He paid the check and walked her to the elevator, his arm around her shoulder. He nuzzled her neck, ignoring the smiles of the few people in the lobby.

"Our luggage?"

"That can wait." H pulled her onto the elevator. They were alone and he whispered in her ear. *"Voy a hacer el amor contigo toda la noche"*

"All night? Really," she said, leaning back against him. *"Eso espero."*

And so they did. It was as if they were the first couple ever to make love.

"Ay, sí," she cried. *"Sí. Sí. Ay, sí."*

"Ay sí, mi amor," he whispered in return. *"Eres mi amor y esa la verdad."* The truth. I do not lie.

In the middle of the night, the door to their room flew open and men burst inside. "Wake up!" one of them said.

Donnie and Cecilia sat up in bed, too startled to speak. They were both naked. Instinctively, Cecilia pulled the sheet up over her breasts.

Donnie jumped out of bed. "What the hell? Get out!"

"Adalgar sent us," the leader said.

The moonlight streamed into the room and Donnie could see there were three of them, in jeans and sleeveless shirts with stocking caps pulled down over their faces. They had the door blocked.

"Adalgar said to tell you that Clay's not coming to any hearing, and if you know what's good for you, you'll never try to contact Clay again."

Donnie started for the telephone. "You've delivered your message. Now leave. I'm calling the police."

The leader advanced menacingly. "You're not calling anybody. Watch him, boys." The two men moved toward Donnie. The leader turned to Cecilia. "The boys told me you were a hot little *tamale.* You're naked under there, ain't you? Why don't you get out of bed and let us have a look?"

The two others held Donnie. "Don't hurt her," Donnie said. "I'm warning you."

"We're not going to hurt her. We just want to have a look at her. Get up, *muchacha.*"

Everything happened quickly, Cecilia getting out of bed and crouching beside it, the leader telling her to stand up so he could see her, Cecilia standing up, her naked body glistening in the moonlight, her arm pointing at the leader.

"You want a look. Look at this." She had a black Springfield XD sub-compact handgun in her hand.

"Wow," the leader said. "The lady's got a pop-gun. You don't know how to use that thing, do you, darlin'? God, you're good looking," he added with a grin, taking in her naked body.

Cecilia didn't hesitate. She fired one shot. The sound echoed loudly around the room. The bullet grazed the top of the leader's stocking cap. "That was a warning. One more word out of you, and the next one will be between your eyes. *Entiendes, pedazo de mierda?*"

The men knocked into each other in their scramble to get out of the room. Donnie could hear them tromping down the stairs and out into the street. Seconds later, he heard the roar of a truck racing madly down Main Street away from the hotel.

Donnie and Cecilia stood looking at each other. Donnie was breathing heavily but Cecilia seemed perfectly calm. "My God, you're wonderful." He looked admiringly at the naked girl. "Where did you learn to shoot like that?"

Cecilia put on the safety and returned the small gun with its three inch barrel to her purse, which she had grabbed from the bedside table and hidden under the sheet in the first confusion of the break-in. "Oh, Donnie, I grew up on a ranch in Guerrero. My father bought me the gun when I came to Texas to study."

They dressed hurriedly. The hotel staff came running upstairs to see what was happening.

Later, they sat in the empty bar, drinking coffee quickly brewed by the hotel manager, and waiting for the sheriff to return from checking Cecilia's concealed handgun permit.

The manager hovered over them. "Are you sure you're all right? Really, are you sure?" He was talking to Cecilia. There was as much admiration as concern in his voice.

She nodded, sipping the coffee and leaning against Donnie.

Thirty minutes later, the sheriff returned. "I don't think those old boys will be filing any charges. Republic Militia, I imagine. All hat, no

cattle. You two are free to go. A clear case of self-defense, it seems to me."
He handed Cecilia her permit. "Thanks for not killing one of them, Miss.
We have enough problem with those idiots without having to go through
a murder investigation."

Cecilia laughed. "I was tempted."

"You're a very good shot. We admire that kind of skill around here.
The grand jury would have no-billed you in a second."

CHAPTER TEN

They were on the road within the hour, eager to get out of Mirabeau. The mountains were dark behind them and the BMW's headlights reflected off the highway. Theirs was the only car on the road. Donnie was driving and Cecilia slowly came down from her adrenaline high.

"It's not often I shoot at someone."

Donnie glanced at her. "Not often?"

"All right, this was the first time."

Donnie reached over and rubbed her neck. Her long hair felt like black silk. "Now that I know you're carrying, you can have your way with me anytime you want."

She sat up and got her cell phone out of her purse. "I need to call Sid Banger and tell him what's going on and see what he thinks we ought to do."

"Cecilia, it's 4:00 a.m."

"He made me promise to call him the minute we had anything to report." She smiled at Donnie. "I should have called him last night, but you had me distracted."

She put her cell phone in the cradle and the sound of the phone ringing came clearly over the car's sound system.

Sid answered his phone immediately. His drawl resonated unpleasantly through the BMW's Logic7 speakers. "Where the hell have you been, Counselor? Is the professor all right? Don't you know the hearing's on Friday?" It was now early on Monday morning. Donnie could almost see Sid's owlish face, thick glasses and acne scarred cheeks.

"Good morning to you, too," Cecilia said. "How's the election?"

Sid sighed. "Too close. Our weekend polling has Payne and Braeswood both with forty-five percent, with ten percent undecided. If this hearing makes it look like we've tried a dirty trick and got caught at it, it could cost us votes and we don't have any to spare. Might mean the election. So tell me some good news."

Cecilia recounted the events of the previous day, including the Militia's raid on their hotel room.

"I see." Sid didn't ask what the two of them were doing in a hotel room in Mirabeau in the middle of the night, but he left no doubt what he thought. "So if I've got this straight, Costin confirmed the professor's story and gave you a statement, but his homo partner won't let him testify. Is that about it?"

"That's right." Donnie spoke for the first time. "But it's a great statement."

Sid interrupted. "I assume you found a notary public and had Costin swear to it under oath?"

"We were in the middle of nowhere, Sid," Cecilia explained. "There was no way. Besides, he promised to be at the hearing in person."

"O.K., O.K., so we have this great un-notarized statement that supposedly clears Professor Cuinn." Sid's voice was heavy with sarcasm. "And we're going to use it to defend an accused forger. Good job, you two."

Cecilia protested. "We did do a good job. Clay really opened up to us."

"Maybe if you two had spent less time in the sack and more time looking for a notary public, it would have been better. Counselor, call me when you get in. Professor, it sounds like you need some rest. I'll see you at the hearing."

Donnie started to protest. "Our lives were threatened, you know," but Sid had hung up.

They drove the rest of the way to Austin without talking much. Donnie tried to think about the hearing, but memories of their night together kept intruding. He hoped Cecilia was having the same problem.

They stopped for gas in Johnson City. Donnie went into the station and brought back two cups of bitter black coffee. He looked at Cecilia. *"Te amo."* She smiled winsomely. *"Lo sé. Yo también te amo, Donnie."*

They made it to Austin for the end of the morning rush hour on MoPac. Cars were bumper-to-bumper heading north into the city. The BMW didn't like the slow speeds, or the stop and go traffic. Donnie was impatient and tired by the time they pulled into the Haven's parking lot.

Cecilia went to her room to shower and change before going to see Sid Banger. "Sid and I have to discuss how to handle the hearing. You get some sleep."

Donnie went into the café to report to Lena and Papa.

Lupe was alone behind the counter, crying.

"What's wrong, Lupe? Where's Lena?"

Lupe sobbed, dried her eyes on the hem of her apron. *"Oh, mi pequeño."*

"What is it? Is it Papa?"

"Not *Señor* Ralph. It's *Señora* Lena. She's very ill. The ambulance came and took her to the hospital. *Señor* Ralph is with her."

When Donnie got to the Sisters of Extreme Charity Hospital and asked for Lena, he was sent to a small waiting room outside the Intensive Care Unit. Papa, Dorrie Louise and a doctor in a white coat were there. The room was a harsh white under fluorescent lights. And it was cold. *So cold,* Donnie thought. He hugged Papa. "How is she?"

"The doctor is just telling us. Come sit here beside me."

The doctor sat on one side of the table, the three of them on the other side. To Donnie, it felt that they were adversaries, fighting over Lena in some way. He distrusted this doctor and he feared what he was going to say.

"Mrs. Rothschild was my first patient when I came to Austin. I've treated her for a number of years for a heart condition. Now, I'm sorry to tell you, she has pancreatic cancer."

"You knew about her heart and didn't tell me?" Donnie asked Papa.

"She did not want to worry you. I'm sorry. We should have told you."

Donnie wanted to say, *you should have called me,* but then he remembered that he had his phone switched off the entire time he was with Cecilia. They had probably tried.

The doctor cleared his throat and went on. "Simply put, the cancer has progressed past the stage where treatment will do much good. And I doubt that her heart would stand it if we tried some heroic treatment. The only way she's alive now is because we have her on life support."

"But isn't there something you can do?" Dorrie Louise wiped tears from her eyes.

"I'm afraid not. The question is whether to discontinue the life support and let nature take its course."

Donnie slapped his hand against his leg nervously. "You mean, let her die?" *He wants us to let her die.*

"It's up to the family of course, but we can make her comfortable so she's not in any pain."

Donnie looked from the doctor to Papa in anguish. "Are you going to let them do this? You can't just let her die."

Papa took off his glasses and wiped them carefully with the handkerchief from the pocket of his tweed jacket. "If you remove the life support, how long will she have?"

"Not very long at all."

"And if you don't?"

"It's impossible to say. Many times, we can keep a person breathing with life support for days, or weeks, even months."

"Would she be conscious?

"That's very doubtful. Her body has made the decision. She is suffering. She is dying. There's nothing we can do to change that. It's a question of how long you want her to struggle."

Papa sighed. "Can you give us a few minutes alone, Doctor?"

"Take all the time you need. I'll be at the nurses' station."

After the doctor left, Papa shook his head sorrowfully. "I believe she would want us to remove the machines and let nature take its course."

"You can't, Papa. You just can't. I can't stand to lose her." He fell into Dorrie Louise's arms, sobbing.

She patted his back. She took his head in her hands and wiped the tears from his cheeks with her thumbs, just as she had when he was little and scraped his knee. "We've already lost her, Donnie. She's already gone."

Papa stood up. "I hope you will do the same for me, Donnie, when my time comes. I'm going to tell the doctor to remove the life support." There were tears in Papa's eyes. "It never occurred to me that she would go first. Not in a thousand years."

Dorrie Louise kissed him on the cheek and hugged him.

Donnie sat with Papa beside Lena's bedside all day and into the evening, listening to her shallow breathing and then, at last, she wasn't breathing at all. He took Papa home and gave him a tumbler of Irish whiskey. "Drink this, Papa."

"Did I do the right thing?" He ran his hand through his carefully combed hair and straightened his tie.

"You did, Papa. You did the right thing." He knew that was what Papa needed to hear. He helped the old man undress and get into bed. When he finally fell asleep, Donnie left quietly. He knocked on Cecilia's door.

She opened the door. There was a worried look in her eyes.

"It's over," he said. "She's gone." He let himself go then and wept.

Half awake, Donnie heard the sound of knocking on his apartment door.

It was Wesley. "D. Ray, are you in there?"

Cecilia got out of bed and put on her nightshirt. She gathered up her clothes from the floor where she had dropped them, rummaged around for her key, and went into the other room. Donnie heard her open the door.

Wesley asked in a knowing tone, "Where's my boy?"

"Your boy is in bed. Donnie, Wesley's here. I have to go."

Donnie struggled out of bed and pulled on shorts and a t-shirt. He hadn't had a thing to drink last night, but he felt like he had the worst hangover of his life. Then he remembered. *Lena.*

Wesley came into the bedroom. He held two steaming cups of coffee in his hands. He put down the coffee and hugged Donnie. "I'm so sorry, D. Ray. She was a great lady."

Donnie nodded. "Thanks. And thanks for the use of the Beemer. Let me get the keys."

"No, no. You use it this week. I've got Cindy's Porsche."

"The Yellow Monster?" Donnie tried to smile.

"The very one. Anyway, I came by to give you some support but I see you're doing O.K. without me." He raised his eyebrows. "I'm proud of you, boy. She's fine."

Donnie smiled. "She is, isn't she?"

Wesley handed him a coffee. They went into the other room and sat at the kitchen table. Donnie rubbed his eyes, trying to wake up.

"From what I hear, it wasn't just a pity fuck either." Wesley grinned. "Stu and Sid tell me that you two made some major magic out in Mirabeau."

Donnie just shook his head. "Does everybody in Texas know my business?" Then he added, "I really don't want to talk about her with you, Wesley."

Wesley grinned. "That's not very grateful. Who taught you how to get in her panties? It worked, didn't it?"

Donnie glared angrily at the bigger man. "It wasn't like that. She's not like that at all."

"Right…. So you didn't tell her what she wanted to hear? You didn't tell her you'd decided Santa Anna was a saint?"

Donnie got up. "Get out, Wesley. I'm going back to bed. Thanks a lot for stopping by."

"Calm down, son. I didn't mean anything. I'm going. Seriously, though, I'm in town, at the apartment. You know the number. Call me if there's anything at all I can do. Otherwise I'll see you at the services." He opened the door. "One more thing . . . "

"What?" Donnie asked wearily.

"Don't lie to yourself. Lie to her, but never to yourself. Remember?"

Donnie shut the door in Wesley's face and went back to the bedroom. He fell into bed, which was full of Cecilia's scent. He loved her. That was the truth.

He woke again late in the morning. He showered and dressed and tapped on Cecilia's door. She was combing her long black hair. She looked at him defiantly with her dark black eyes. "What did Mr. Bird want?"

"Just offered condolences; told me to keep the Beemer for the week; congratulated me on my girl friend."

She bristled. "He used those exact words, I'll bet."

Donnie smiled. "Well, not quite."

"I hate it when Wesley Bird talks about our private life."

Donnie agreed. "Me, too. But Sid knows we slept together. I imagine Sid told Stu and Stu told Wesley."

"*Bastardos.*"

"He seemed happy for us, if that's any comfort."

"It's not."

He took her hand. "Let's go see how Papa is doing."

Papa was up and dressed, almost his old self. He had taken charge of the funeral arrangements with the same *savoir-faire* he had shown in dealing with the press. The funeral was to be the next day, at the State Cemetery. The arrangements were coming together just fine, he allowed.

Donnie was surprised to see Dorrie Louise in the kitchen.

She had a white apron over a floral dress. "I've come to help, as long as Papa needs me." She was standing over the stove, cooking some kind of meat dish.

"Donnie, your mother is a wizard of the kitchen."

"Goodness knows I've had enough experience. We'll keep the café open except during the services. People who live here need a place to eat."

Donnie kissed his mother on the cheek. "What does Grover think about this?"

Dorrie Louise smiled mischievously. "You know, I didn't ask him. I will tell you that he won't be at the funeral."

Donnie's spirits lifted a little. "Why not?"

"He can't afford to be seen with you. Blackcap vireo and that land thing, you know. He's frightened that General Payne will find out you're related."

"We're so not related. Does this mean I'll never have to see him again, or is this just a temporary reprieve?"

"Oh, Donnie Ray." Dorrie Louise laughed. "You're such a card."

Papa looked at his notes, written in his precise hand. "I've made enough calls for now. Tell me about the hearing. Tell me what happened in Mirabeau."

Papa and Dorrie Louise listened and laughed, as Donnie and Cecilia described their exploits in the mountains.

Dorrie Louise hugged Cecilia and said, "You shot his cap off his head? That's the grandest thing I ever heard." If it bothered her that Donnie and Cecilia had been in the same hotel room, she didn't show it. Donnie already knew that Papa approved of the Mexican law student.

"So what happens on Friday?" Papa asked.

Cecilia explained. "It looks like the hearing will go ahead. Donnie will have to testify. The A.G.'s men have been looking high and low for him to serve their subpoena but it doesn't matter. He will appear and tell what really happened and we'll dress up Clay Costin's affidavit and submit it."

"Without it being sworn to?" Donnie asked.

"We have no choice. It wouldn't be admissible as evidence in a regular trial, but this isn't a court. You'll testify what Clay told you. It's hearsay, I know, but we'll try. If necessary I'll testify that I heard it too. The question is whether that will outweigh whatever Drury has to say."

"In the press," Papa said.

"Yes. And with the undecided voters."

"Let's hope that it does." Papa turned back to the phone and the plans for Lena's funeral.

Donnie stood with Papa at the entrance to the white stone chapel that overlooked the State Cemetery on Navasota Street in East Austin. Below them, to the right, were rows of crosses precisely marking the graves of Texans who died in the War Between the States. On the hillside above the crosses, were markers of all sizes and elaboration, where prominent Texans were buried.

"Papa, it's really beautiful here. How does Lena qualify to get buried in the State Cemetery?" He pulled at the sleeves of the new black suit that Cecilia had insisted he buy from an upscale re-sale shop she knew about.

Papa smiled his gentle smile. He also was dressed in black, in a suit Donnie had never seen before. They both wore black ties and had small red roses in their lapels. "Do you remember Manny Horace, or was he before your time?"

"The Speaker of the House?"

"Yes, for several terms. But I'm speaking about long before that, when he lived at the Haven Hotel. He was always late on his rent. He never had enough money to buy books. Lena worried that he didn't eat enough."

Donnie led Papa out of the bright sunlight, to a spot under the arbor that separated the chapel from a service building where caterers where preparing food and a group of musicians were getting their instruments out of their cases. "Let me guess. Lena waited on the rent, and gave him free food, and money for tuition and books."

"That was Lena." Papa steadied himself and gazed down at the clear stream that ran over a rocky bed, between large oak trees, to a pond in the center of the cemetery. "It happened with Manny every term. He came from poor people. What they could send him just wasn't enough. He worked all the time, all the way through law school, but he never had enough money. Lena saw him through, right up until he passed the bar exam."

Papa looked up at the street, which was filling with cars. The black hearse that had brought Lena's body from the funeral home was parked in the drive next to the chapel. "They're coming." He paused to shake the hands of a young couple. Donnie recognized them as Haven residents.

Papa turned back. "When Manny became Speaker, one of the first things he did was call Lena and ask her if she and I would like burial plots in the State Cemetery. Of course, he had long since paid back all the money he had borrowed. He said she deserved to be here if anyone did. Our plots are right over there." He pointed to a shady rise on the north side of the cemetery. "Not too far from Sam Houston's son, Andrew Jackson Houston, you'll be happy to know."

Donnie smiled. They greeted the mourners. They had formed a long line that stretched from the chapel to the street. It seemed every person wanted to share an anecdote about Lena's generosity or her humor. Papa laughed softly and listened carefully. He introduced Donnie to each one… a Texas Supreme Court justice, a former mayor of Austin, a well-known newspaper reporter, a retired general, the former Chancellor of the University of Texas, and dozens of other, more ordinary folk, who told them how Lena had touched their lives. Cecilia came in, kissed Papa and Donnie, and took a seat near the back of the chapel. Wesley hugged them both, whispered something in Papa's ear, and sat down near the front.

It was time. Papa and Donnie led Dorrie Louise and Lupe to the front of the chapel to the row marked for family. The musicians took their places in front of the mourners. Their leader was Jacky Jaxson, the famous country and western singer. Donnie remembered watching Jacky play on *Austin City Limits,* the PBS television program broadcast from a studio on the University of Texas campus.

Jacky tuned his guitar and said to the crowd, "This is a little tune that Lena always liked." He launched into the plaintive melody of his early hit, "I Hate To Say Adios." It was a song about a lost love, but on this day, it was as if it had been written to say goodbye to Lena.

Donnie wiped tears from his eyes and put his arm around Papa, who was sobbing quietly. As the last chords died away, there was a hush over the room.

Papa sighed and made his way slowly to the podium. He unfolded a piece of paper, covered with his neat handwriting. Twice he tried to read what he had written, but each time he stopped and tried, unsuccessfully, not to sob.

"Let me, Papa," Dorrie Louise said. Donnie was relieved. He couldn't have done it.

With a clear bell-like voice, his mother read the poem that Papa had written for his beloved Lena.

"Why did you choose me, Maid of my Youth?
You looked at my tray, beans and toast, and said,
You must have more than that, filling my plate
With fruit and meat and sweets of all kinds.

"You blessed me, Maid of my Youth –
In our marriage bed and little home, you said,
You must have time to work, filling my heart
With joy and kindness and sweets of all kinds.

You aged with me, Maid of my Youth –
When I complained of growing old, you said,

We will always have each other, filling my life
With memories and reveries and sweets of all kinds.
But now you have left me, Maid of my Youth –
To whom will I speak, and what will I say?
A life without you, what does it mean?
Just the recollection of sweets of all kinds.

A collective sigh went through the room as Dorrie Louise finished. She sat beside Papa and kissed him on the cheek.

There were prayers by an Episcopal priest and by a Methodist minister. There were remembrances by the famous and the ordinary people who were there. But all Donnie heard was the wail of sorrow and pain, of Jacky Jaxson's song and the loneliness of Papa's poem.

He hardly noticed being served with a subpoena by Mt. Everest, the larger goon from the Attorney General's office, ordering him to appear before the Senate committee at Friday's hearing.

Cecilia snatched the subpoena out of Donnie's hand and turned on the hapless investigator. She pulled him by the arm outside the cemetery gate. Donnie could hear her swearing at him in Spanish until the man pulled down his Stetson hat and scrambled away, saying, "I'm just doing my job, ma'am."

After the services ended, Wesley took Donnie aside. "I'll swing by and pick you up, say about ten? You think Papa will be in bed by then?"

"I don't think so, Wesley. Cecilia and I need some time together."

Wesley frowned. "Well, bring her if you want to, but Cindy says that Anna Kaye really wants to see you again. Stu's bringing his current lady. The six of us can have a wake down at the Warehouse, raise a few to Lena's memory."

Donnie thought a second. "I'll ask Cecilia. If she wants to, we'll see you down there."

Wesley smiled. "If she doesn't want to, you come anyhow. I'll be sure Anna Kaye's there, just in case."

Donnie had taken Cecilia to a club crawl with Wesley and Cindy before. She hadn't liked it then and refused to go the next time he asked her. "Too many stories about you two getting into trouble. Too many sexist, racist, obscene jokes."

"Is that all?" Donnie asked kiddingly.

"No, Also, too much booze and too many cigars. Not to mention being groped by Mr. All American."

Danny pretended he didn't care. He teased her, "Wesley was just being friendly."

"Is he that way with all your dates?"

"I don't know. I never had one tell me before."

"You're pathetic."

So Donnie didn't mention Wesley's invitation to Cecilia when they got back to the Haven. He had a twinge of regret when he remembered The Acrobat, but then he looked at Cecilia sitting beside Papa, reading condolences from the stack of sympathy cards they had brought home from the service. The fullness of her breasts under her black dress, the sound of her slightly accented voice, the way she glanced over to him and smiled, put Anna Kaye right out of his mind.

CHAPTER ELEVEN

Papa sent them away; he wanted to be alone, to compose his thoughts and memories of the day. *Another poem is in the offing,* Donnie imagined.

Cecilia collected a bottle of wine from her room and they settled in on Donnie's couch, sipping wine and talking about Donnie's testimony.

"Good wine," Donnie allowed, brushing back a lock of hair from Cecilia's forehead.

"It should be," she said. "It's a Cabernet Reserva from my father's friend's winery. My father is a wine connoisseur."

"I thought he was a rancher."

"Rancher, wine lover..."

"Sire of beautiful, armed women." Donnie stretched and yawned. "Isn't that enough preparing?" His hand fell on her shoulder and he nodded toward his bedroom. *"Podemos ir a la cama ahora?"* he asked, leaning over to kiss her.

"No. There's plenty of time for that. First, the hearing."

"Pero después, haremos el amor, si?

"Quizá," she answered. "Later."

They were going over Clay Costin's affidavit and how Donnie should present it when there was a loud knock. "D. Ray. Open up. It's Wes."

"Be quiet and maybe he'll go away," Donnie whispered. He had forgotten that Wesley had a key to the apartment. "Oh, God," he said when he heard the door being unlocked.

Wesley waltzed into the room, Cindy under one arm and Anna Kaye under the other. Cindy had a bottle of vodka in one hand. Anna Kaye was balancing three plastic glasses in her hands. She put them down on the counter and squatted in front of the refrigerator. Her shorts could not have been shorter. *The Acrobat.*

She pulled out the ice trays, set them in the sink and turned to Donnie and Cecilia.

"I love what you've done with the place. And in such a short time." She extended her hand to Cecilia. "I'm Anna Kaye Nordstrom."

"This is Cecilia," Donnie said. She took Anna Kaye's hand and nodded to her.

"So I gathered," the tall girl replied.

"My lawyer."

The three intruders laughed.

"We're on our way to the Warehouse," Wesley said. "Didn't he tell you we're having a wake down there tonight, Cecilia?"

Cecilia didn't reply.

"We're busy, Wesley," Donnie said.

"I'll bet." Wesley grinned.

"Getting ready for tomorrow. The hearing."

"Piece of cake. You can handle those old boys. Sid will be there. Not to mention your very attractive lawyer." He sat down beside Cecilia. He looked at the bottle of cabernet. "*Reserva.* Very nice." He poured himself some wine in Donnie's glass and sipped it. He held the glass up to the light and then looked at Cecilia suggestively. "Nice body." He finished the glass and stood up. "So tell me, what's the plan of action? Tomorrow, I mean. I think I can figure out tonight."

Cecilia spoke to Donnie, ignoring the others. "Your lawyer is going to retire now. Try to get a little rest before the hearing."

Donnie went with her to the door. "Don't go."

"Play with your friends." She left.

Wesley, Cindy, Anna Kaye and Donnie sat on the covered patio of the Warehouse, with Sid Banger and a buxom girl whose name Donnie never got, well into their second round of oversized Martinis. The Warehouse was an upscale Martini and cigar bar just west of Congress Avenue, in a section of downtown Austin undergoing rapid gentrification. A guitarist and his piano accompanist were playing soft Western rock.

After toasts to Lena, Donnie recounted the trip to Mirabeau. The more he got into his story, the more he drank, taking gulps of the Martini as he got to the climax of the adventure.

"She really has a fucking handgun?" Anna Kaye asked.

"Damn right; she still does." Wesley blew a large circle of cigar smoke in the air and winked at Donnie. "Knows how to use it too, right, D. Ray?"

"Damn right."

The table went silent. Donnie supposed the girls were imagining the slender Mexican girl taking aim at the intruder. He knew that he was. What Wesley was thinking about, he didn't want to know.

The talk turned to the election. Wesley ordered another round of drinks. "Yeah, Braeswood's going to make it. I really believe he is."

"I hope so," Cindy said. The former cheerleader snuggled up against Wesley. "After the election, Wesley and I are getting married."

Donnie gaped at Wesley. "Is this true? Is the big man going down? Married?" He turned to Cindy. "You're a brave girl, to try to make a married man out of this crud."

Wesley lifted his glass, clinking Cindy's glass. "To us, sweet pants."

Donnie sipped his drink. "You said, after the election. What's the election got to do with it?"

"Nothing, nothing," Wesley said. "That's just the date, is all."

Cindy sighed happily. "Anna Kaye will be my maid of honor. And Wesley wants you to be his best man."

"That's right, D. Ray. I couldn't get married without you there."

Donnie agreed of course. He didn't mention the three engagements he had watched Wesley break, including one on the day before the wedding. Amazingly, Wesley was still on good terms with the three girls and their families. Donnie suspected any one of the three would marry him in a heartbeat if he asked her.

Donnie accompanied Wesley to the cigar vault. While Wesley looked at the cigars, Donnie asked, "What's going on, Wes? Are you really going through with it this time?"

Wesley chose Cohiba Maduros for the men and Lonsdales for the girls. He handed one of the Cohibas and his cigar cutter to Donnie. "That's an antique. A gift from Cindy."

"Very nice." Donnie cut the tip off the long dark cigar.

Wesley took the cigar cutter back and worked carefully on his cigar. "I always meant to get married, but when the time came I couldn't see spending that much time with any of them. Cindy's different."

Donnie leaned over the flame of Wesley's silver and gold lighter. He drew contentedly on the cigar, inhaling the fragrant tobacco. "How different?"

Wesley smiled at him through the air, heavy with cigar smoke. "Well, her monthly income is $100,000. Her mother is the largest shareholder in one of the largest oil companies in the United States."

"You never told me that. Let's have another drink. This wedding may actually happen."

Several rounds later, Wesley tossed the keys to Cindy's Porsche to Anna Kaye. She grabbed them in mid-air.

The Acrobat still has it, Donnie thought with hazy admiration.

"Will you drive Donnie home, A.K.?" Wesley asked. "Cindy and I are going back to the apartment. We'll take a pedicab." The bicycle taxi for two had become popular in downtown Austin. They were everywhere, a threat to both pedestrians and cabbies.

"Sure." The Acrobat staggered to her feet. "Ready, lover?"

Donnie was feeling equally woozy. He had drunk enough that he didn't object to the tipsy girl behind the wheel of the Porsche.

They got in the car and she drove with the exaggerated slowness of the really intoxicated. They avoided the main streets as best they could. Donnie laughed and said "Turn here . . . No, wait, turn here . . .No, not there . . .Here." He doubled up with laughter when they ended up in one dead end and then another.

Somehow they got to the Haven. Anna Kaye retrieved her overnight bag from the back of the car.

Donnie swayed and steadied himself with one hand on her shoulder. "You staying?"

"Damn right." She was really slurring her words now. "You owe me a fuck. I don't like that Mexican woman. The one with the gun."

They crept quietly down the corridor that led to Donnie's apartment. When they passed Cecilia's door, there was no light showing under the door. "Sssh," Donnie whispered.

They staggered to his apartment. Donnie opened the door and turned on the light. Anna Kaye sank down on the couch and took off her shoes.

Donnie tried to explain that she couldn't stay, but the words kept coming out garbled, and Anna Kaye didn't seem to be listening anyway. She was trying to unbutton her blouse, but her fingers kept slipping off the buttons.

Donnie managed to say, "Wait right, right here." Slowly, he made his way back up the hall to the office. He pulled down the guest register. It slipped out of his hands and landed with a noisy plop on the floor. He picked it up carefully and finally focused enough to see that the room next to his apartment was unoccupied.

He could hear Papa snoring softly in one of the two the bedrooms behind the office. Donnie was struggling to find the key to the vacant room when Dorrie Louise came out of the other bedroom.

She had pulled her robe tightly around her. "What in the world is going on? Are you all right, Donnie Ray?"

He explained that there was a girl in his room who needed a place to stay. It took several tries and it was a garbled explanation, but when she finally understood him, Dorrie Louise acted as if it was the most normal thing in the world, and that maybe this is how things were done in the big city. She found the key and walked with Donnie back to his apartment, steadying him when he leaned too far one way or the other.

Anna Kaye was sound asleep on Donnie's couch.

"Poor thing," Dorrie Louise said. "Do you think she's all right?"

"Probably had a little too much to drink," Donnie offered.

"Oh. Well, let's get her into her room."

Together, they got the sleeping girl off the couch and into the vacant room. She mumbled a little, but didn't wake up. They deposited her on the bed. Donnie went back for her overnight bag and shoes and handed them to Dorrie Louise. She shooed him away. "You go to bed. I'll take care of this."

CHAPTER TWELVE

The next morning, Anna Kaye tapped on his door. Donnie was awake, hung over but awake. She was dressed and carrying her things. He had on his shorts. "Bye, lover. Did we have a good time last night?"

"The best."

He looked up and saw Cecilia coming down the hall. Anna Kaye smiled mischievously and grabbed Donnie around the neck and kissed him. When he finally managed to free himself, Anna Kaye turned to Cecilia. "He's all yours." She strutted down the hall and out the door.

Cecilia shook her head. "Get dressed."

Donnie started to explain, but she walked away, saying over her shoulder, "We need to leave in fifteen minutes. Wear your good suit."

She was sitting impatiently in the Yaris when he came out of the hotel. "Get in," she said. "We're late."

"We can take the Beemer."

She ignored him.

"You can drive."

She shook her head with pity. "Just get in the car."

She had on a black pin stripe suit, jacket and skirt, with a white dress shirt, the sleeves turned back over the cuffs of the jacket. "I never saw you in your go-to-court clothes before," he tried.

She continued to ignore him, her face steely. She backed out of the parking lot and drove toward MLK.

"Cecilia, just let me explain."

She glanced over at him, barely missing a group of students in the crosswalk. "No, thank you."

Donnie took his cell phone off his belt and texted a message to her. It read:

Nothing happened last night. You can ask Dorrie Louise.

Her phone rang and she read the message. They stopped at the intersection of MLK and the Drag. She texted him back.

When his phone rang, he read her message:

Ask Ur mother if U slept with Brunhilde? No thx.

He wasn't sure what to say to her. At the next intersection, she texted him:

Did U tell her you luv her in Swedish?

"For God's sake, Cecilia. She's not Swedish. She's from Waco."

They drove the rest of the way in silence. She parked in a garage two blocks from the Capitol building. He followed her to an elevator. She punched the down button angrily. When the door opened they were in a tunnel. She walked hurriedly down the tunnel. Donnie tried to keep up but he kept looking around, wondering where they were. Cecilia seemed to know where they were going. They came out of the tunnel into what appeared to be an underground part of the Capitol building.

"What is this?" he asked.

She kept walking as she explained curtly, "This is the top floor of the four story underground extension to the original Capitol building that was built in 1993. They didn't want to disturb the approaches to the original building, so they built this."

"What all's down here?"

"Offices and meeting rooms." They entered a circular area. "The rotunda is right above us. This is supposed to mimic it, upside down."

"That's bizarre." Donnie craned his neck to look at the globe.

Cecilia walked ahead rapidly, her high heels clicking with authority on the polished stone floor. He followed her. They came to Committee Room 105A. It was 9:30; a notice outside the door said that the hearing was scheduled for 10:00 a.m.

"Cecilia, will you just listen?"

She turned on him, hissing, "Forget all that. Concentrate on your testimony. *Entiendes?*"

"*Si,*" he answered miserably.

They went into the large committee room. Sid Banger, skinny, with shaving nicks on his pockmarked face, waved wearily at them. He stood by a long dais at one end of the room. He had on a rumpled suit, a flowery necktie and a shirt that hung loosely around his scrawny neck. He was looking up through his dark glasses at a tall, stout man with thick gray hair, dressed neatly in a blue suit.

The dais extended in a semi-circle with seats for ten senators. Computer monitors were in front of each senator's place. Before the dais was a small table and chair, with a mike.

"The witnesses sit there," Cecilia explained.

For the first time, Donnie felt butterflies. He was going to have to sit in that chair and tell his story to people who might not believe him. He wished he hadn't drunk so much the night before.

A State employee was adjusting microphones and a TV technician was setting up a camera in the back of the room. Donnie recognized the blond reporter, Christine Newby, standing beside the camera. She wore heavy make-up and her conservative suit didn't hide her fantastic figure. She smiled at him and waved her microphone, inviting him to be interviewed.

He shook his head. *No thanks,* he mouthed. He and Cecilia took seats at the right front of the room, next to the witness chair.

A crowd was gathering outside the committee room. Donnie knew he could have prepared better. This has the appearance of being serious. He was going over his statement one more time, feeling more and more unready for the ordeal, when he looked up and saw a familiar face pushing through the crowd and past the uniformed guard at the door. Donnie recognized the shaved head. It was Clay. He was dressed neatly in a gray suit with a blue shirt and red tie.

"Don, sweetheart," he said loudly. "Am I on time?"

Donnie had never been so glad to see anyone. They embraced. He looked over Clay's shoulder at Cecilia and shrugged. *Well, at least someone wants to have sex with me. Hell, I'm so happy to see him; I might just do it.* Clay reluctantly turned loose of Donnie and kissed Cecilia on the cheek. "Annie Oakley!"

"We thought you weren't coming," Cecilia said. She motioned for Sid Banger to join them.

"After you scared the shit out of the Militia? Oh, girl, you're the hero of Mirabeau. I love you so much it's almost enough to make me go straight. I told Adalgar I was coming to this hearing and that was that. I also told him if he tried anything else like that hotel stunt, he'd never see this ass again." He patted himself on the rump.

Cecilia introduced him to Sid. Clay smiled and held his hand out to Sid. "Here I am, all dressed up and ready to save the day."

"Great to see you. Let's go over here, where we can talk." He and Cecilia each took one of Clay's arms.

Don't let him get away, Donnie thought.

"You stay here," Sid said to Donnie. Donnie watched them take Clay into a corner of the room. The three of them conferred quietly. Clay looked up and smiled happily at Donnie. In a few minutes, they rejoined Donnie. Cecilia leaned down and whispered in Donnie's ear. He caught her familiar smell, *perfume or soap or whatever.* It was clean and crisp and flower-like. It was Cecilia.

"Listen to me," she said. "We needed to hear straight from Clay, what he'll testify to."

"Is it all right?"

"*Si, es perfecto.*"

What a relief, Donnie thought.

Sid took Cecilia by the arm. "Come with me. We need to talk to Marcus."

"Who's Marcus?" Donnie felt a little left out of things.

Sid was impatient. "Marcus is Senator Tompkins' Chief of Staff." He and Cecilia went back to the dais. He motioned to the stout man in the blue suit Sid had been talking to earlier. Sid began talking softly to Marcus. Cecilia was listening intently.

Interested people crowded into the committee room, taking almost every seat. Looking out at the crowd, Marcus motioned for Sid and Cecilia to follow him through a door behind the dais. He held the door for Cecilia and the three of them left the room.

Donnie and Clay sat silently for a minute. "Nervous?" Clay asked.

"Absolutely. Aren't you?"

"Of course not. It's like a performance. I love to perform." He glanced across the room, to the opposite front row. "Well, well. Look over there. Do you recognize my boss?"

State Archivist Jonathan Drury was talking to two men who looked like lawyers. Drury was thin, with a receding hairline and sharp features. He wiped his brow and looked nervously around the room.

"Watch this, if you want to see a grown man sweat." He pranced over to Drury and shook his hand. Then he leaned in close and showed Drury a small black object he had taken out of his pocket. He whispered in Drury's ear, then turned triumphantly, winking at Donnie, and made his way back to his seat.

Drury whispered to the two men, nodding nervously in Clay's direction. Clay had been right. Drury was sweating profusely. One of the lawyers hurried through the door behind the dais.

Donnie leaned over and whispered to Clay. "Whatever you said to him seems to have worked. They don't look too happy. What was that you showed him?"

"Oh, this? I told him it's a microfiche of Archive records from the 1920s. I told him that I am here to testify for you and that we have iron-clad proof."

"Where did you get that? Is it for real?"

"You don't want to know." Clay smirked.

"Does it have anything at all to do with the Payne documents?" He waited and Clay smirked again. "You were bluffing him, weren't you?"

"He's not that hard to bluff."

Ten o'clock came and went. The crowd settled into place. *Apparently most legislative hearings don't start on time,* Donnie noted. Some bystanders wandered out and tried to bring coffee back into the room. The security guard made them leave it outside. The guard directed some others, twitching from nicotine withdrawal, to the outdoor smoking area at the far end of the corridor.

Wesley and Stu Short arrived and found seats behind Donnie. Stu was dressed in his journalist's uniform, jeans, a polo shirt and a corduroy jacket. He was six inches shorter than Wesley, but he still handled himself like an athlete. Donnie remembered that Stu had been a place kicker for the Longhorns when Wesley made All-American.

Wesley had on still another Italian suit of the lightest wool. His handmade English shoes shone under the fluorescent lights. He whispered in Donnie's ear. "Did you and A.K. set off fireworks last night?"

Donnie hissed back. "No, but we torpedoed my relationship with Cecilia just the same. Thanks a lot."

Wesley grinned. "I didn't force you." He whispered again, with a knowing grin. "Want me to tell you how to get her back?"

"Get out of here." He thought a second, then smiled. "Better still, I want you to meet Clay Costin, our star witness. Clay, this is Wesley Bird. One of the few admittedly gay football players ever to make All-American."

Clay turned in his seat and looked admiringly at Wesley. "I love football players."

Wesley mumbled something and Donnie said, "Keep Clay happy, will you, Wesley? He's vital to our case. Keep him relaxed and happy. I have to go pee."

When Donnie got back, Stu had disappeared and Wesley had his head in his hands, while Clay chattered merrily.

Another half hour went by. Cecilia, Sid and Marcus finally came back and sat down beside Donnie and Clay. A stocky man followed them into the room and took his seat at the center of the dais.

"That's Senator Tompkins, Payne's stooge," Clay said under his breath.

Tompkins' blue pinstriped suit stretched tightly across his shoulders. He had a whispered conversation with a clerk, who adjusted the microphone. The senator's jowls shook when he talked. The other chairs on the dais were empty. He thumped the mike with his finger. The clunk echoed through the room. The crowd quieted down, waiting expectantly. The TV cameraman turned on his strobe light. Tompkins looked washed-out in the bright light. He had not bothered to put on make-up. He blinked in the harsh light, then leaned into the microphone and spoke. "This hearing has been postponed indefinitely." He stood up and turned to leave.

"Senator Tompkins," Donnie heard Christine Newby shout, "does this mean we won't know what's true and what isn't before the election?"

He left the room without answering.

Reporters swarmed around Marcus. Christine was heading their way. "Refer all questions to Sid," Cecilia said to Donnie and Clay. "Better still, come with me." Hurriedly, she led them through the door behind the dais, apparently off limits to reporters, and down a long hallway.

"But what about my testimony?" Clay complained. They walked to the end of the corridor. There was an exit to the main hall.

Cecilia opened the door and looked out. "All clear." She turned to Clay. "You scared them into adjourning the hearing. That ought to be satisfaction enough." She grabbed him by the shoulder and kissed him on the cheek.

"I suppose so." Clay tore himself free from Cecilia's grasp, "I need to find that football player," and headed back to the conference room.

"No interviews!" Cecilia shouted after him.

He twiddled his fingers at her and began his search for Wesley. *He'll need his best open-field moves to escape Clay,* Donnie thought

Donnie looked questioningly at Cecilia. "What happened? Did the idea of Clay testifying scare them that much?"

"Not exactly. Sid can tell you the details."

Sid joined them, Wesley in tow. *Apparently he had outrun Clay.* They ducked into an empty conference room. Sid explained, "The Payne people could see that the hearing might turn out really bad for them. Drury's a nervous wreck. He just looks like a liar. You and Clay have your stories straight. On the other hand, it might go bad for us. Clay's a loose cannon. And the press might seize on words from Drury like 'forgery' and 'planted.'"

He lit a cigarette and grinned. "So...we reached an agreement with the Devil: Tompkins calls off the hearing and we pull the ads. No more ads showing our Payne imitator running around drunk, chasing a Mexican general in a dress. There's still two weeks until the election. Payne hopes the voters will forget the ads, and we hope they'll remember them."

"I was surprised that Payne agreed," Cecilia said.

"It was nip and tuck," Sid admitted. "Bob Braeswood signed off on the deal, on my advice of course, but it took Tompkins and Marcus forever to talk Payne into agreeing. He was dead set on having the hearing, wanted to remove the stain on his good name and so forth. That's what took so long." He turned to Donnie. "You're a free man, Professor."

Donnie sighed. "I have to say I'm relieved."

Cecilia shook hands with Sid. She turned to Donnie. "Congratulations, Donnie. I'm sure Mr. Bird will give you a ride home." Then she was gone.

Stu took Donnie, Wesley and Sid to lunch at the Press Club, a luncheon club on the top floor of a prominent Austin bank building. "One of the few

privileges of being a journalist." He had reserved a private room. It had full windows from which the Capitol was visible to the north and the Highland Lakes to the west.

Wesley laughed and said to Donnie, "The john's around the corner. It's got urinals with a view. Take a look."

Donnie went in, and sure enough, the urinals were built with windows above them, looking to the west. Donnie could see the noon hour traffic on the MoPac expressway. He could almost make out the roofline of *the Haven. Cecilia's probably there now. What* is she doing? How can I make her understand? he lamented.

Above the washbasin was a full-sized painting of a nude Marilyn Monroe. He admired the nude, but his thoughts kept returning to Cecilia in his arms, in the hotel room in Mirabeau. He was relieved he didn't have to testify, but if testifying had meant she would still be there, he would have gladly done it. *Somehow, I'll convince her that we are supposed to be together, that I meant it when I told her I've changed. God, I love her.*

He washed his hands and splashed cold water on his face. *Was that it? Was it all over?* For some reason he doubted it, and he wished that Cecilia was going to be beside him. He felt he was going to need her even more than ever. But why, he couldn't say.

When he returned, Stu had ordered drinks from the waiter. While they drank, Sid reviewed the campaign. "Payne's still strong in West Texas and the Panhandle. There's no way they would ever vote for a Democrat. Braeswood has the Hispanic vote in the Valley and San Antonio, and of course the labor vote on the Gulf Coast and the liberal vote in Austin. He has a chance to get the Bible Belt vote in East Texas. Those yellow dog Democrats want an excuse to vote Democrat, and the ads might give them one. We'll probably split there. That leaves the white middle class vote in the Dallas-Fort Worth and Houston metro areas. Those have been solid Republican for a long time, but Payne's not their type. He's too old fashioned, and the ads make him a laughing stock. Your upward mobile white voter doesn't look kindly on fools. Still…" he paused.

Stu finished his thought. "...Have the ads run long enough?"

"That's the question. And that's what we won't know until election night. Meanwhile," Sid said, raising his glass in a toast, "keep your toes crossed and pray to the patron saint of elections."

Donnie raised his glass. "Who would that be, exactly?"

"Why, St. Chad, of course." Sid grinned.

It was a long lunch, and it was 3:30 in the afternoon before Stu dropped Donnie and Wesley off at the Haven. Donnie gave Wesley the keys to the BMW. They watched Stu drive away. "I'm afraid I've lost her."

"Lost who?" Wesley twirled his car keys.

"Right. You know who. Cecilia."

"What happened?"

Donnie sighed. "Anna Kaye and I were so drunk we didn't know what we were doing, but I wasn't so drunk that I could sleep with her, not feeling the way I do about Cecilia. I put her in a vacant room. Dorrie Louise even helped me. Of course, wouldn't you know, when Cecilia came to get me this morning, Anna Kaye was telling me goodbye. When she saw Cecilia, she gave me a big kiss, just for spite. Plus, I was mostly naked."

"Are you telling me that Cecilia won't believe you when you say you didn't sleep with A. K., is that it? Just because she saw you naked, kissing her? How unreasonable can a girl be? It must be some Hispanic thing."

Donnie nodded sadly. "I did have on my shorts."

Wesley put his arm around Donnie's shoulder. "You know all this, but let me explain it to you one more time."

"Please don't."

Wesley ignored him, "First off, it's a mistake to tell her you didn't fuck A.K. She isn't going to believe you anyway."

"As always, you're a big help."

"I can get her back for you."

"Don't," Donnie said. But he listened anyway.

"Just admit everything, but tell her you had to get A.K. out of your system, you know, a farewell fuck; say it wasn't even that good, because Cecilia was all you could think about. Girls love to hear that, even when they don't believe you. I can't tell you how often I've used that line."

"I'm not going to lie to her."

"You have to lie to her. It's for her own good. She doesn't want you to say you didn't sleep with A.K. You're either dishonest, or worse, you're a weakling for turning down a woman like A.K, which, by the way, you are."

Donnie laughed. "I don't believe a word of that and neither do you."

"You were weak, D. Ray. All the more reason you need to be strong now. Go in there and lie through your teeth."

Donnie left Wesley carefully checking the exterior of the BMW for any signs of damage. Waving despondently, Donnie went directly to Cecilia's apartment, not sure what he was going to say or how he was going to convince her to listen to him. The door was open and Lupe and Dorrie Louise were stripping the bed. Their mop and bucket and vacuum cleaner were blocking the door. Donnie stuck his head in the door. "Where's Cecilia?" He dreaded the answer.

Dorrie Louise looked up at him. "She's gone. She checked out two hours ago."

Donnie flinched. "Gone? Where did she go?"

"I don't know. She just put her things in that little car and left." She turned to Lupe. "Did she tell you where she was going, Lupe?"

"Mexico. She said she was going home."

Donnie had no idea where in Mexico she might be going. He knew she had the offer of a job with a Mexican law firm when she finished her studies in the States. That was all he knew.

"You can find her, Donnie," Dorrie Louise said. "There has to be an address somewhere, at the law school maybe."

He sighed. "It doesn't matter. I'm afraid she's left me forever."

142

CHAPTER THIRTEEN

Donnie spent the two weeks until the election partying at night with Wesley, Cindy and Anna Kaye. He tried to fuck The Acrobat enough times to chase away thoughts of Cecilia, but it didn't work. He spent most days sleeping at Wesley's apartment or playing Angry Birds on his phone. He only went home to get clean clothes. He couldn't stand being at the Haven without Cecilia.

Also, Dorrie Louise warned him not to bring Anna Kaye back to the Haven. "You picked the wrong girl, Donnie Ray. I don't think I can be civil to her, because I know that your soul mate is in Mexico."

Donnie kissed his mother on the top of her head. "Give it up. It's hopeless. Cecilia's through with me."

A few days before the election, Wesley woke them up early. He shooed the girls out of the apartment. "Sawbucks is flying in. Get dressed, D. Ray. Try to comb your hair."

"Why don't I just leave too? It's a lot less trouble."

"Go, go," he said to the girls. He closed the door behind them. "I want you to meet Sawbucks. I've told him about you. I think he may offer you a job."

"A job? Doing what?"

"Doing what I'm doing. Schmoozing investors."

Donnie frowned. "I don't think I'd be any good at that. I'm no football star. Who wants to talk to a historian?"

Wesley laughed. "It doesn't matter. I can teach you everything you need to know in about thirty minutes."

"I doubt it."

"Just meet him. Keep your options open."

Donnie finally agreed. He showered and put on a clean white shirt and pressed jeans. He combed his cowlick and presented himself to Wesley for inspection. Wesley had on a shirt and tie.

"It'll have to do." Wesley had an edge to his voice that Donnie hadn't heard before. The house phone rang and he ran to answer it.

He's nervous, Donnie realized. *I've never seen him nervous before, not about anything.*

"Thanks, Geraldo." Wesley hung up the phone. "Geraldo always calls me when Sawbucks shows up, so I don't get surprised."

"Sawbucks doesn't approve of Cindy?"

"Oh, he likes Cindy all right. He's a friend of her family—but he wouldn't want to know if I had another girl up here."

"Don't ask, don't tell?"

"Exactly. You and I think exactly alike."

Yeah right.

They waited for Wesley's employer to appear. To pass the time, Donnie had done an Internet search on Sawbucks Banjo. There were numerous entries about the controversial oilman. He was a geologist with a degree from a small Kansas college. He had started out drilling oil and gas wells with funds provided by his friends and relatives. He had scrounged for prospects passed over by the major oil companies as too small or too risky; Sawbucks tied up those prospects with a lease from the landowner, giving him a sixty or ninety day sight draft, ostensibly to check the landowner's title to the oil and gas rights, but really to give himself time to find financing for the deal. If he couldn't sell the deal, he would simply tell his bank to return the sight draft. The landowner had no recourse, because the sight draft was payable at Banjo's option. After he hit a few wells, it became easier for Sawbucks to find backers. Usually he sold the entire interest in a lease, retaining a carried interest, which meant Sawbucks had to pay none of the costs or bear any of the drilling risks; the investors paid all the costs and took all the risks and Sawbucks got an operator's fee and shared in the revenues after the investors recovered their investment. It was a formula that gave Sawbucks some income, whether the well produced or was dry. A few times, investors sued him, claiming that Sawbucks had sold 125% or 150% of a well, counting on the well being dry or on his ability to renegotiate the deal if the well hit. Sawbucks loved litigation and he usually won.

After ten years or so, Sawbucks had enough income from his carried interests that he could expand. He hired his own land man to deal with the property owners and began to invest some of his own money in his projects. But there was always a pattern of Sawbucks having little of his own money at risk in a well; he always had the maximum interest with the least amount of risk that he could squeeze out of a deal. Over a couple of decades Sawbucks had built a moderate size oil company, which he took public during one of the periodic oil booms. His shareholders expected greater returns than Sawbucks could generate and the stock price stalled until Sawbucks got into the greenmail business.

He teamed up with a famous Wall Street corporate raider and, using Sawbucks' knowledge of the business, they began acquiring stakes in troubled oil companies, threatening to make tender offers, but always selling out for a profit when the company decided it was better to pay them off than to put up with the aggravation. Sawbucks seemed set, but the next oil bust sank his share price. In one of his rare mistakes, Sawbucks had invested his own money in his own company's stock. He barely survived, struggling along on the fringes of the industry, showing up at seminars and on cable television programs to promote his drilling funds. But then oil and gas prices recovered again, and Sawbucks moved on from drilling wells to speculating on energy prices.

Having predicted the most recent upturn in oil prices, he acquired a reputation as an expert on the movement of energy prices. Whenever oil prices reached a new peak, Sawbucks was on the business channels, predicting another one hundred dollar increase in the price of oil. Even oil price declines did not dampen his enthusiasm or, apparently, his reputation. He ventured into alternative energy projects, raising money for tar sands gasification projects in Canada, solar energy in the Arizona desert, wind turbine farms off Nantucket, tidal wave power generation off New Jersey. With his *Energy For the Future Fund* and his *Alternative Energy Is the Answer Fund,* he raised billions of dollars from investors. His fund management fees provided him millions in income, and in the unlikely event one of his projects was successful, he had retained the usual Sawbucks Banjo carried interest.

Sawbucks Banjo's business was raising money, and one of his chief lieutenants in that effort was Wesley Bird, Jr., who stood by the door anxiously waiting for the man who provided the good life.

The door flew open and the man himself stormed in, carrying a garment bag over one shoulder. "Hey there, Birdman," he said to Wesley.

Birdman? Donnie thought. *Never heard that before. That will be worth its weight in gold.* He looked to see if Wesley was embarrassed that Donnie had heard the nickname, but the football player was too busy taking Sawbucks' bag and pouring him a single malt Scotch on the rocks.

Sawbucks Banjo was a senior citizen look-a-like of Alfred E. Neuman, but with a florid complexion and a perpetual scowl to go with his buckteeth and unruly hair. He turned to Donnie. "Who's this?"

Wesley introduced him. "My lifetime friend, Don Cuinn. I told you about him? A possible recruit for Investor Relations?"

"Oh, yeah. 'Lo." He waved at Donnie dismissively. He turned back to Wesley. "Birdman, we need to talk about the LeSaul investment. I said I wanted five out of him and all he signed up for was three."

"Not to worry, Sawbucks. The other two million is on its way."

"Are you sure?"

Wesley answered rapidly, too rapidly. Donnie could see he was winging it. "One million for sure."

Sawbucks held his glass out to Wesley for another drink. "No. Five. You told me he was good for five. When did you talk to him last?"

Wesley poured the drink and handed it back to Sawbucks. "I'm talking to him all the time. He just has to free up some mutual fund money."

Sawbucks held his glass up and stared through its crystal prism at Wesley. "Call him. I want the rest of that money in our bank by tomorrow afternoon. I'm not paying you to chase pussy all around Austin. I'm paying you to raise money, so do your job. I need a shower." He went into the bedroom that had been kept locked, fresh for the tycoon whenever he happened to be in Austin.

When they were alone, Wesley shrugged. "Back to work."

"I'd better go." Donnie gathered up his things from the hall closet.

"I'll call you when he leaves." Wesley reached for his cell phone. He pressed a speed dial. "Mr. LeSaul," please. Tell him it's Wesley Bird." He grinned at Donnie, his old confidence showing again. "Piece of cake."

"Good luck, Birdman." Donnie hurried through the door ahead of Wesley's foot.

Donnie took the shuttle bus back to the campus and hiked the rest of the way to the Haven. He was in no hurry. He thought about Wesley and Sawbucks, trying to imagine what it would be like to work for Sawbucks Banjo, raising money. It was an unsettling picture.

When he got home, he went into the lobby. Papa was sitting in the small library, a card table in front of him. On the table were several stacks of papers and an open metal box. "What's all this?" he asked Papa.

Papa looked up at him soulfully. "Lena's papers. I have to go through them. I'd rather be water boarded." He shook his head and stared at the piles.

"Can I help?"

"No, no. Thank you, but it's my duty, and I will perform it, I suppose." He thumbed through some of the papers. "Look at this. Her bank statements, her checkbook. I know nothing about all that. Lena did everything of that sort." He sighed. "She sheltered me from all this grubby, practical mess. All I had to do was write. Everything is different now, without her."

"It is different, for us all." Donnie sat down and started to try to organize the papers.

"Leave it, Donnie. We need to have a conversation."

Donnie obeyed. "Of course, Papa." He waited for the old man to begin.

Papa cleared his throat nervously and then began. "First of all, I need to apologize for not being more of a father to you." Donnie started to protest, but Papa went on. "It's true. I know myself. I know I am remote from other people. I was glad when Lena told me she wanted to keep you here to raise, after your mother, well, you know of what I speak."

Donnie nodded. "I know, but Papa, you were kind to me, always. And you taught me to love books and to respect education."

The old man sat back in his chair and stared out the window. "Perhaps. But as I was saying, I was glad when Lena said she wanted to raise you here. I was glad because Lena was so happy and because she and I had never had children. Sadly, though, I did not know how to be a father, perhaps because I never had a father myself, or a real mother for that matter. Maybe that's why I have always taken such refuge in my work. And I thank God that I found Lena, or rather that she found me, because she understood me and gave me a cloistered place in a noisy world. Exactly what I needed."

"What happened to your father and mother, Papa? You've never mentioned them before."

Papa took out his pipe and tobacco pouch. He filled the bowl with the familiar nutty Cavendish tobacco. The soft caramel scent of the tobacco filled the room. Papa puffed on the pipe for a few minutes before he went on. "I never told you about them, because it is very painful for me to talk about. Now, I think I owe it to you."

He took another puff from his pipe. "I was born in Alsace, but I spent my first years in a village called Montignac. It's on a beautiful river called the Vezere. Man has been there forever. Some of the oldest wall paintings in Europe are there. Just before the fall of France, at the start of the Second World War, my father moved our family there from Alsace to escape the Nazis. Alsace was not safe for Jewish families like mine. Montignac was in Vichy, the unoccupied part of France."

"Were there other Jewish families there?"

"Before the war there were only a few Jewish families in all of the Dordogne and then several hundred of us descended on the area. But the locals welcomed us, found the men jobs, kept us safe."

"Then what happened?"

"Well, the Nazis kept pressuring the Vichy government to round up the Jews. My father saw that we needed to get out. He was a doctor. He had some connections and some money left. He was able to get tickets for my mother and me on the last freighter to leave Marseilles. Sadly, there was no room for him, so he sent us off by ourselves. He promised to join us in Cuba."

"Was he able to?"

"No, I never saw him again. I imagine he died in a camp, but I have never been able to find out for certain."

He wiped his eyes with his handkerchief and then went on. "We got to Cuba just before the Cubans stopped accepting Jews, which probably kept my father from joining us. Then while we were in Cuba, my mother took ill and died from pneumonia. Family friends, the Steins, took me in and we finally got to Galveston, here in Texas, where I grew up."

"Were the Steins kind to you?"

"Oh yes, very kind. But they were older, their children were grown, and I was mostly on my own." He went on. "I taught myself English by reading poetry and I've been a poet ever since."

"Papa, I'm so sorry, about your family, I mean—"

"Thank you, Donnie. I tell you all this so you may understand better why I was not a better father to you. I did not know how."

"I don't agree, Papa. You've been wonderful."

"No. I've been remote. I remember when you were first in school, how unhappy and alone you seemed. You had very few friends, do you remember?"

"I do, Papa." Donnie recalled himself as a small boy, standing by himself on the playground, wondering why his mother had abandoned him.

"Then later, you came out. It was then when you needed someone to guide you, to teach you the importance of always doing your best. I did not do that. What did I know about a child like you? Even though, in a way, we were both orphans. I should have known. I should have showed you the way."

He went on. "When you got to high school and then to college, I thought maybe you would end up with a life much like mine, alone with your inner life and your study of history. You had no father; you only saw your mother from time to time. You must have felt abandoned."

"I quit worrying about it. Besides, I had you and Lena."

Papa's eyes brightened. "Ah yes, Lena. Lena believed that you could do no wrong. She never saw the frightened little boy that I saw. She wouldn't hear there was any problem when you seemed to quit caring. Lena was even happy when you fell in with Wesley."

"You weren't?" Donnie was surprised.

Papa paused. Finally he gathered his thoughts. "No, I wasn't. I was glad you had a close friend, an active social life, girls, good times, things I never had, and that I knew you needed." He paused before going on. "You have a real knack for scholarship, you know. Deep down, I know there is an essential honesty about you. But there is a disregard for others in Wesley, and sometimes I have seen that in you as well, and I have not been glad about that."

"You never said anything."

"I had no right to say anything. You had grown up under my roof and I had left you to face the world the best you could. That failure of mine eradicated any right I had to judge your conduct. And we all know that Wesley can be very charming. I've felt his charm myself. God knows he charmed Lena."

Donnie reached out for the old man's hand and held it between his own. "Papa, don't blame yourself. I've turned out all right, haven't I?"

Papa squeezed Donnie's hands. "Have you? Take this San Jacinto article. Are you proud of its scholarship, or its intellectual integrity?"

Donnie bristled a little at the unfamiliar criticism from Papa. "Why shouldn't I be? It's true." But then he remembered his conversations with Cecilia and he forced himself to admit, "No. You're right. It's not very good, is it?"

"I'm afraid not. A true scholar would have sent it to authorities in the field for their comments. He would have sent the galleys to a professional publication for review before it was printed. Instead, you sold it to a magazine for use as a political smear. Are you proud of that? I'm not."

Donnie was silent. He could think of no answer.

"I thought I saw a difference in you when you and Señorita Medina were together. I think she brought out a better side in you."

Before Donnie could answer, he went on. "The reason I say all this now, is to ask you what you intend to do next. You can stay here, of course. There will always be a place for you here."

"I will stay if you need me, Papa. I would never desert you."

"No, no. That is not a consideration. Dorrie Louise has promised to stay on, as long as I need her. It's you I'm worried about. What would you really like to do?"

Donnie hesitated, searching for the words to express what he had been trying to work out in his mind ever since Mirabeau, and especially ever since Lena's death and Cecilia's departure. "What I would really like to do is study Texas-Mexican relations, go to the original sources and tell the full story, present both sides."

Papa nodded in agreement.

Warming to his idea as he talked it through, Donnie went on. "Take Santa Anna. It's easy for an American to say he was a dictator who was bad for his people. But the fact is that the people accepted him, time after time. Why? There had to be reasons they followed him. It may have just been that he represented the best hope they had, a poor hope as it turned out, but the best one they had, to live free of complete domination by us. I'd love to dig into the original source documents and paint the picture of the two countries in the Nineteenth and Twentieth Centuries, from the Mexican perspective, for the serious American student. And not just Mexico. All of Latin America. My Spanish is good enough. I think I could find a lifetime of work there."

Papa smiled gently. "More than one lifetime, I imagine. So why don't you do it?"

"First, I have to get a job. After things quiet down, and I've saved some money, I will do it. I promise."

They sat quietly. Donnie could tell that Papa was thinking about what Donnie had said.

Dorrie Louise came into the room. She had on an apron and was holding a dust cloth in her hand. She saw the papers on the card table. "Come on, Papa." She pulled a chair up to the table. "We need to get this mess organized." She leafed through the stack of papers. "I've been running a business for twenty years. This won't take long." She looked up at Donnie. "Go take a nap. You look awful."

Donnie grinned. "So you're in charge now? For the first time, I feel sorry for Grover." He winked at Papa, who winked back.

She threw her dust cloth at him. "Scat. We have work to do."

CHAPTER FOURTEEN

Sunday afternoon before the Tuesday election, Wesley showed up at Donnie's apartment. "God, get me a beer, quick!" Wesley plopped down on Donnie's couch.

"That bad, huh?" Donnie handed Wesley a Corona.

"I've been listening to Sawbucks' bullshit ever since I saw you last." He took a long swig of the beer. "Do you know why he's called Sawbucks, instead of Chauncey, which is his real name?"

"The ten dollar bill story?"

"Right. And it's true. He really does have the first ten-dollar bill he ever swindled an investor out of. It's in a frame on his desk. He looks at it every time he has to part with a dime." He drained the beer and handed the empty bottle to Donnie. "I've raised a hundred million dollars for that horse's ass, and he still treats me like a hired hand. I can't wait to get out of there."

"And do what?" Donnie handed him another beer, opened one for himself and then joined him on the couch.

"Something will turn up."

"I've been thinking about what you said the other day, about a job?"

"Yeah," Wesley answered. "We need to talk about that."

"I've tried to think it through. The thing is, I don't believe I could work for Sawbucks. It's not my thing, you know?"

Wesley laughed. "That's just as well. Sawbucks turned you down."

Donnie leaned his head back on the couch and sighed. "So much for taking a stand on principle, academics over filthy commerce."

"Was that it? Or were you afraid you couldn't hack it, you worthless crud?" Wesley grabbed the remote and turned on Donnie's television. "God, what a small screen," he complained.

"Oh, it was the principle; it was definitely the principle."

They settled back to watch the Cowboys play the Giants.

The game was in the first quarter, a scoreless tie, when the first commercial break came on. Donnie was in the bathroom losing some beer, when he heard Wesley let out a whoop.

"D. Ray, come here quick! Look at this!"

Zipping up his jeans and hurrying back, he was in time to see the familiar figure of the Payne impersonator stumbling drunkenly across the San Jacinto battlefield, chasing a fleeing man in a woman's dress! Accompanied by the damning words, intoned by the whiskey voice of Jacky Jaxson: *Sam Houston didn't trust the first Sam Payne. Should you trust this one?*"

"What happened?" Donnie shouted. "I thought Sid made an agreement with Marcus. No more ads if Tompkins adjourned the hearing."

Wesley grinned happily. "I'd say Marcus just got double-crossed. It's too late for Tompkins to re-open the hearing now. The election is on Tuesday."

"So Sid went back on his word? Can you just do that? Will anyone believe him next time?"

Wesley rummaged around in Donnie's kitchen cabinet and found a bottle of bourbon. He poured them both stiff drinks. "If Braeswood wins, that's all anybody will remember. Sid's a fucking genius." He handed Donnie the whiskey. "I knew the race was razor thin close. This could swing it. Drink up and let's count how many times they run the damn thing."

They stopped counting at twenty, during the second half of the Sunday doubleheader. They switched channels and the ad was on everywhere they checked. It was saturation bombing. Wesley and Donnie drank and laughed at what must have been happening at Payne's headquarters.

Donnie spent Monday and Election Day Tuesday applying for a teaching job. The postings outside the dean's office had a number of next semester openings for history instructors. He was determined to get a job. He was pretty sure his chances with colleges in Texas were not good. *Leaving Austin might be a good thing,* he considered. He updated his C.V. and e-mailed it to five different out-of-state schools. He wrestled with how to disclose the Payne magazine article and finally decided to list it under "Other Publications." He hoped that the personnel officer of the Four Corners Community College in southwestern Colorado was not following the Texas gubernatorial election.

CHAPTER FIFTEEN

There were election night parties all over Austin. Wesley, Cindy, Anna Kaye and Donnie drank Mojitos and watched the returns on the flat screen in Wesley's apartment at the Timeless, which was crowded with election watchers. Several were Sawbucks' investors, with their girlfriends or trophy wives. Wesley introduced Donnie to Pierre LeSaul. The reluctant investor, tall, dark-skinned, with a Gallic profile and a faultless tailor, shook Donnie's hand disinterestedly. Donnie resisted the urge to ask LeSaul if he had come through with the additional two million dollars. He decided he really didn't care.

All the pundits, temporary celebrities the local TV stations had scraped up from UT's Government Department to assist the local news anchors, agreed that the last minute media blitz from the Braeswood campaign had made the race too close to call. They said that Payne's responses were too timid, trying to cast Payne as a statesman and criticizing mudslinging. The pundits agreed that coming from Payne, it wasn't particularly believable.

The pundits thought that the ads had not cost Braeswood much Hispanic support. The Spanish language ads he ran in Hispanic areas were completely different.

Payne was running strong in the East Texas Bible Belt. The big unknown was how the white suburban voters would go. Would they desert the Republican candidate or not? Early exit polling in the suburban precincts showed significant questions about Payne's character, but also dismay at Braeswood's mudslinging. No one could tell how the two concerns would balance.

The crowd got rowdier as the night went on. Early returns from small towns in West Texas came in first and Payne jumped to an early lead. Christine Newby was covering Payne headquarters at Austin's famous Driskill Hotel, where supporters in gaudy Western wear yelled with pleasure and danced to a Western band. But then Braeswood boxes from labor districts on the Gulf Coast brought him back even with Payne. The Braeswood campaign had taken the Austin Convention Center for its election night party. Braeswood's supporters shouted anti-Payne obscenities and mugged for the TV cameras.

There was a buzz coming from the apartment entry hall. Through the crowd, Donnie could see Sawbucks Banjo, with his Alfred E. Neuman grin, shepherding Bob Braeswood into the room. The candidate was taller and more slender than Donnie had expected. He had on a politician's dark blue suit and red tie. His salt and pepper hair was carefully parted and razor-cut. He leaned down and grasped the elbow of each person Sawbucks introduced. He whispered in their ears, laughed at their jokes, expressed delight in seeing them; in short, he worked the room like the pol he was.

When he got to Wesley, his face lit up and he hugged him. "Wes, my man. How are we doing?"

Wesley laughed and patted the candidate on the back. "You're a shoo-in, Governor."

"No, no. Not 'Governor.' Not yet. Don't jinx me."

"O.K., but it's true. You're going to win." He pulled Donnie forward. "A big reason I'm so sure is this young man. Congressman, meet Donnie Cuinn. He wrote the Sam Houston article."

Braeswood leaned back and looked at Donnie appraisingly. "So you're the scholar who found out the truth about my esteemed opponent. Let me shake your hand."

Donnie mumbled something inarticulate that he hoped was modest enough.

Braeswood winked. "We need to talk. After the election. I want to hear the whole story."

Donnie mumbled again and Braeswood turned away. He kissed Cindy on the cheek. "Tell your folks I said hello." He hugged Anna Kaye, *too long*, Donnie thought and then he and Sawbucks were gone.

The lead bounced back and forth all night. About two in the morning, the crowd drifted away. Cindy had already gone to bed. Anna Kaye kissed Donnie and staggered sleepily into their bedroom. By four o'clock, only a few die-hard political junkies remained with Donnie and Wesley. The commentators looked tired of repeating the same stories over and over. Even Christine Newby looked like she needed a good nap.

Donnie stretched, waved at Wesley and went in the bedroom. He undressed and lay down beside the naked Anna Kaye. She turned to him sleepily and he fell between her athletic legs, but neither one's heart was in it.

About eight o'clock, Wesley woke him up. "Get up, D. Ray. They've called it for Braeswood, buddy. We won."

"Took long enough." Donnie yawned. "Has Payne conceded?"

"He's about to. I thought you'd want to see it."

Donnie pulled on his pants and went in the living room. They sat alone in front of the television set. The familiar pudgy face of the Attorney General appeared on the screen. The usually perfectly coiffed hair was not quite perfect. The make-up was slightly smeared. For what was probably the first time ever on television, he had his glasses on. He might have been drunk. Those of his campaign workers still at the Driscoll tried to chant, "Payne, Payne, Payne," but it was a weak effort. He raised his hands, the room fell silent, and he read his statement.

"I've called Mr. Braeswood to congratulate him on his victory. I told him how distressed I was by his campaign's gratuitous slanders of my family, and he assured me that he had nothing to do with it. That is all I will say."

He turned and left the platform.

Braeswood on the other hand spoke for twenty minutes to an enthusiastic crowd at the Convention Center. He thanked Payne for his "gracious telephone call," but otherwise did not mention him at all.

Revenge is best served cold, or at least not with a world class hangover, Donnie thought. So much had happened. He had expected to feel different, watching Payne concede. Mostly he felt relief that it was over, and regret that Cecilia wasn't there with him.

"Where's Sawbucks?" Donnie asked.

"After he came up here with Braeswood, he did the same thing at a suite at the Driscoll with Payne. He gave serious money to both campaigns. He'd never be caught not backing the winner. Then he got in his plane and flew back to the real world in Dallas. You can bet he's already figured out how to leverage Braeswood's victory into some advantage for Sawbucks Banjo." He switched off the TV. "Let's go get some breakfast, D. Ray. We've got plans of our own to make."

Pedro's Mexican restaurant on East Seventh Street, in the heart of the barrio, had been the favorite breakfast hangout for Texas pols for decades. By the time Wesley and Donnie got there, it was already filled with red-eyed, unshaven men and a few frizzled haired women, all laughing and reliving the excitement of the election, and trying to guess the effect on themselves of the Braeswood victory. Who would be who in his administration? How much support would he have in the legislature?

Wesley ordered them migas and coffee at the counter. Pedro, Jr. himself, the grandson of the first Pedro, poured them coffee. It was dark, black and hot. Waiting for their order, they looked around the room.

"Lookee there," Wesley said, nodding at Sid Banger and Marcus deep in whispered conversation in one corner. "Bygones will be bygones, I guess."

Sid looked up, saw them, and waved.

They took their plates of eggs and found a table on the side patio. Mexican girls scurried around in the early morning air, carrying baskets of chips and bowls of Pedro's famous salsa. Another girl put a full pot of coffee on their table and smiled. "You happy with the election?"

"*Mucho*," Wesley said.

"*Si*," she answered. "Payne es un culero."

"*Si, un verdadero culero.*"

"*Si, si.*" The girl laughed and hurried off.

They ate hungrily. Between bites, Donnie said. "I sent off resumes to some out-of-state colleges yesterday. One of them looks pretty promising."

Wesley put down his fork and stared at Donnie. "Why would you want to do that?"

"It's pretty simple. I need a job."

"But our man won. You can do a lot better than some junior college. You're going to come to work for me."

Donnie shook his head. "Sawbucks turned me down, remember?"

"No, no. I'm through with Sawbucks. I want you to come work on my campaign."

"Your what?"

"My campaign. For Congress." Wesley grinned at Donnie's befuddled look. "I'm running for Bob Braeswood's seat in Congress. Cindy and I are getting married and moving to Corpus Christi and I'm filing for Braeswood's seat as soon as he resigns."

"Whoa, wait a minute. What did you just say?"

Wesley leaned back in the wooden chair and grinned. "I'm running for Congress. Think about it. It's a natural. I'm super photogenic and very attractive."

"I especially like your modesty."

Wesley took a big bite of migas, then said, "Plus, I am well acquainted with a large group of wealthy people who would love to see me in Congress."

"You mean Sawbucks Banjo's investors?"

160

"Exactly. Just think about it, D. Ray, you and me in Congress."

"So they have Co-Congressmen now?"

"Well, no. I'd be the one who would actually take the oath. But you would be right there with me. You and me, Crud. It's the next step in The Deal."

Donnie looked at the grinning football player. "You're serious."

"I've never been more so."

"You've been planning this and never said a word about it before? You're unbelievable."

Wesley pointed at the figure stumbling out onto the patio. "Here comes Sid. He thinks it's a good idea. I've asked him to be my campaign manager."

The owl-faced campaign strategist staggered across the patio. He blinked in the morning sunlight. He smelled of whiskey and stale cigars. He was still drunk. "There they are. The Dynamite Duo."

"Sit down, Sid, before you fall down. I was telling D. Ray that I'm going to run for Bob's seat. Have you decided to manage my campaign?"

Sid fell into a chair and propped his elbows on the table. He smiled happily. "Let's enjoy the moment, Wes." He took a flask from his pocket. He poured out Donnie's water and filled the glass with whiskey. He took a large swallow. "The Dynamite Duo."

"Right," Wesley said. "Can't you picture it? The three of us together again, in another campaign? Who are the Republicans going to run? That furniture salesman from Weslaco? Hell, it'll be a cakewalk."

"Could be." Sid finished the glass of whiskey and handed the empty glass to Donnie with a wink. "You might not even need any dirty tricks. You better have some ready though; you never know." He grinned slyly at Donnie. "Be Prepared, that's the Boy Scout Marching Song," he sang off key. "Do your research, Professor, be ready, hit 'em when they don't expect it, play offense."

Donnie shifted more upwind from Sid. "How does Marcus feel about you double-crossing him?"

"He's not happy that I outsmarted him. But he's a bright guy. Payne is finished. He's a laughing stock now. So Marcus needs a spot to land. He wants a job in the Braeswood Administration. He wants to be press secretary." Sid giggled. "I told him I'd recommend him. Of course, it'll just be assistant press secretary, but after he's waited around, wondering for a couple of weeks, he'll be glad to get that. Marcus knows how the game is played."

He stood unsteadily and patted Donnie on the head. "You know how to play, too, Professor. That was a good job. You two pulled off as good a dirty trick as I've ever seen. Bob owes you. Anything you want, you let me know. Bob will do it." He pointed unsteadily at Wesley. "Within reason, of course. Wes here's going to marry a rich girl and be a Congressman. Bob thinks that's fine. What do you want? How about State Archivist? Would you like to be State Archivist?" He giggled again. "Just kidding. Too obvious." He handed Donnie his card. "Private number on there. You call me when you decide and I'll make it happen. Sid Banger always pays his debts." He wandered back inside.

Wesley got up quickly and headed toward the toilet.

Donnie felt his anger rise and his face get red. He clenched his fists and banged them on his knees. "I'm an idiot. A fucking idiot."

Wesley finally returned. "Are you all right?"

"No, I am not all right." Donnie said loudly.

"Quiet, keep it down."

Donnie managed to lower his voice. "Sure. We wouldn't want anybody to hear about the biggest dirty trick in Texas political history, would we? Braeswood owes me? What does Bob Braeswood owe me for?"

"Sid's drunk," Wesley said lamely.

"So drunk he told the truth, right?"

Wesley didn't reply.

"Tell me the truth, Wesley. Remember, we can lie to anybody else, but we don't lie to ourselves, do we? And Rule One of The Deal, what was it? It's you and me, together to the end, against the rest of them. Remember?"

There was a long pause before Wesley finally answered. "It worked, that's the main thing. It worked for the two of us. But if I'd have told you, it never would have worked. You weren't strong enough to pull it off, if you had known. I did it for both of us, D. Ray."

"Right. But how? How did you do it?"

Wesley smiled ruefully. "Actually, it wasn't that hard. Stu had the fucking paper. He found it in some collector's estate; the heirs didn't even know it was there. He bought it in a batch of stuff for practically nothing. There it was, Sam Houston's own account of what a cowardly bastard Payne's ancestor was. The Hero of San Jacinto! Stu's always been a big Braeswood supporter. He showed it to Sid and they decided they had to use it. Braeswood's campaign couldn't just release it. Nobody would take it seriously. But suppose it was found in the Archives! Sid was laughing with me about this crazy idea and naturally I thought of you and your thesis.

"Naturally."

"Whatever. Anyway, we decided to salt the Archives."

"Where I would find it." Donnie shook his head. "Did Philby know?"

Wesley shook his head. "No. Not that it would have mattered. Stu has that fairy wrapped around his little finger. He loves big bad football players. But no, Philby did not know."

"So it's a fake then. Sam Houston's account of Captain Sam Payne's actions at the Battle of San Jacinto is a fake?"

"Who knows? Stu doesn't know. I certainly don't know. It could be genuine, D. Ray. Does that make it any better?"

"Not a bit," Donnie admitted. "How did you plant it in the Sam Houston journal? How did you make sure I would find it?"

Wesley smiled. "Remember your friend Clay Costin?"

Donnie groaned. "Clay planted it?"

"That's right. Remember Geoff, that fairy who guides Philby around?"

Donnie nodded.

"Turns out he's Clay's in-town boy friend. He convinced him to do the actual salting. It wasn't hard. All he had to do was put the document in a book from Sam Houston's library and make sure you saw it. He thought you would never notice. He brought it to you five times, in books you asked for, before you finally spotted it. He was like a kid at Christmas when he called Geoff and told him it had finally happened."

"And Stu? What's his cut?"

"A big scoop for the magazine, one that makes it very hard for Drayton Philby to get along without him."

"What about Clay's microfiche, the one he scared Drury with?"

Wesley whistled. "That was totally unscripted. The little bugger wouldn't leave well enough alone. It was a microfilm copy of some other Houston papers. It had nothing to do with Payne."

"What did Clay get out of all this?"

Wesley grimaced. "A back-rub from Geoff, of course. Plus, I got him an audition with a Broadway producer. He thinks he's an actor."

"That was it?"

"Well, I also had to convince Pierre LeSaul to buy one of that Dutchman's sculptures for his garden. That was the hardest part of all."

Donnie stared at Wesley. The truth was sinking in and it was hard to take. "All that crap about The Deal. I should have known. You told me all along to look after Number One, and that's what you were doing, weren't you? I was your patsy and if I got hurt, or Lena and Papa got hurt, it didn't matter, because you're going to be a U.S. Congressman."

Wesley grimaced. "Not just a Congressman, D. Ray. That's just the beginning. Two terms in Congress, then the Senate, and then, who knows? I want you with me, all the way to the top, just like we said. You and me, all the way."

"I'm supposed to believe that?"

"Yes. It's The Truth."

"The Truth," Donnie said with distaste. He sat for a few seconds, then said, "Give me the keys."

"To the Beemer? Why?"

"Just give me the fucking keys. I need to take a ride."

Wesley tossed the keys to the BMW on the table. "Sure. Take a ride. Cool off. You'll see that I did the right thing. We saved Texas from Payne and I'm going to Washington. I'll get a ride back to the Timeless. I'll meet you there."

Donnie scooped up the keys. He went out the patio gate. "He'll get the check," he told the waitress, pointing at Wesley. Wesley waved at him, a hopeful smile on his face.

Donnie gunned the BMW out of the gravel parking lot. He turned the radio up as high as it would go. When he got to the Haven, he put the top down and retrieved his bike from the outside storage closet. He tossed the bike in the back seat. He heard the bike frame rip the soft leather. He drove rapidly toward Old Bull Creek Road. In ten minutes he was at the Coyote Hill gate. It was locked. Backing up, he drove at it at full speed. When he hit the gate, he could feel the bumper give and the headlights crack. He kept his foot down on the gas pedal and the gate finally split apart. He backed up and drove over the gate, dragging the bumper with him.

When he got to the edge of the cliff, he got out of the car and took out his bike. He put the Beemer into neutral and gave it a quick shove. It went over the cliff, slowly at first, then picking up speed. It hit a large rock and bounced in the air. The open door came off. He watched the car flip and land upside down at the bottom of the hill. There was no fire, just a pile of German auto parts.

He threw the keys down the cliff and stared at the wreckage for a long time. "There. So much for The Deal."

He got on the bike for the long hilly ride back to town. It was a steep climb up the first hill and by the time he got to the top and began the exhilarating descent, his head was clear and he knew what he needed to do next. He pedaled around Austin on the 360 Loop, down through Westlake Hills, across the low water bridge, and then downtown. The ride had taken over an hour but he was not tired at all when he got off the bike in front of the *This Texas* offices.

CHAPTER SIXTEEN

The receptionist looked up when he came in, but before he could say anything, Donnie was at Drayton Philby's door. He entered without knocking. The blind publisher was on the floor, dressed in a workout suit, doing crunches. Geoff was helping him, holding down the heavy man's legs.

"We need to talk," Donnie said.

"It's Don Cuinn," Geoff said, helping Philby to his feet.

"I know who it is," Philby said querulously. "Didn't your stepmother teach you any manners?"

Donnie repeated, "We need to talk."

Philby sighed. "Well, come in, then. You sound distressed." He motioned to Geoff, who led him to the leather chair by the window.

"I am distressed," Donnie admitted. "I'm sorry to burst in like this. Can we talk privately?"

"Of course. Geoff, please excuse us." He turned to Donnie. "Shall I get Stu in here?"

"I'd rather you didn't."

"Ah," Philby motioned to his young aide. "Geoff, we do not want to be disturbed. By anyone. Do you understand?"

Geoff looked crossly at Donnie. "Of course, Drayton, if you're sure you'll be all right."

Philby waved his hand in dismissal. "Go, go." When the door snapped shut, he said to Donnie, "Tell me. What is it? I love secrets."

"You may not love this one. May I sit down?"

Philby pointed impatiently at the chair across from him.

Donnie sat down, took a deep breath and told Philby all that he knew about the Payne document.

Philby squirmed uncomfortably in the leather chair. Finally he said, "So you're telling me that Stu Short and Wesley Bird . . . and Geoff . . . planted the Payne expose in the State Archives?"

"I'm sorry to say it, but yes, I am. Wesley told me as much. They used Clay Costin to do the salting, and they used me to do the rest of the dirty work."

There was anger in Drayton Philby's voice. "Those fools. I've spent a lifetime building the reputation of this magazine. This is unforgiveable."

Donnie waited.

"Give me Costin's number. I have a private investigator who can be quite ruthless. We'll want a statement out of Costin. That shouldn't be too hard. Then I will have to confront Stu and Geoff, and discharge them both. There are plenty of journalists who would salivate over the editorship of my magazine. As for Geoff, that little queer can go hustle on Sixth Street for all I care." Warming to his task, he went on. "I doubt that the story will ever become known. Payne will retreat to West Texas like his ancestor and shouldn't bother civilized people again. Braeswood's people certainly won't talk about it. But when I fire Stu, they will know that I know. That should be of some use to me down the road. We'll scare Geoff so he'll never breathe a word."

Donnie could almost see the wheels turn as Philby calculated how to use the information to his best advantage.

The publisher continued. "It never hurts to know something incriminating about a politician. Braeswood's as unscrupulous as any other politician, I fear. What a sorry mess."

"Did I tell you that Wesley intends to run for Braeswood's Congressional seat and that Braeswood is going to endorse him?"

"Does he really?" Philby smiled for the first time. "We can't have that, can we? I believe I can guarantee that Bob Braeswood will never endorse Wesley Bird for Congress. I doubt that he will want to incur my wrath, just for a football player."

"Even so, Wesley has campaign pledges from all of those investors he's been romancing for Sawbucks Banjo."

"Oh, that's rich." Philby laughed. "The most important thing in the world to Sawbucks is his investors. He will listen when I tell him that I know enough on Wesley Bird to embarrass him and his investors, things that Wesley did when he was on Sawbucks' payroll. What's more, I know many of those investors. I will explain to them that Wesley is not an appropriate candidate. That's all I'll have to say."

Donnie listened. "Wesley's always been my friend. I suppose I should feel bad about watching him go down in flames, but…"

"It is necessary. Do you agree?"

"I do agree. Besides, it's not as if Wesley is going to suffer very long. He's marrying Cindy Patson."

"Really? Anne Morgan Patson's daughter?"

"I suppose so. The oil heiress."

Philby burst out laughing. "Really! How marvelous! Old man Morgan left everything to his only daughter. That's Anne Morgan. She married Phil Patson. She's had him on a large allowance and a very short leash for thirty years. I can see it now. She'll explain to her only daughter, Wesley's Cindy, how that's done. Between the pre-nup and the personal assistant who'll report his every movement to Cindy's Mama, and Anne controlling the checkbook, I'd say Wesley's days as a free man are over. Phil Patson told me one day over a Scotch that you don't leave the Morgan family. You just stand there and let them cut your nuts off."

Philby stood and shook Donnie's hand. "Leave everything to me."

On the way out of the building, Donnie's cell phone rang. There was a message from Wesley:

Call me. Stu says U R with Philby. What's going on?????

Donnie turned off the phone and dropped it in the recycling bin on the way out of Philby's office.

Donnie was exhausted when he got back to the Haven. He went straight to his apartment, showered and changed into a fresh pair of jeans and a clean shirt. He checked his emails and saw that the Four Corners Community College was interested in a history graduate with a master's degree who was also fluent in Spanish. He was replying when there was a tap on his door.

"Come in, it's open."

It was Papa and Dorrie Louise.

Donnie turned the laptop toward them. "Look at this. I may be going to work in Durango, Colorado. The college looks pretty nice. Not Austin, of course, but…"

Papa looked at the screen. "You may want to wait to on that, until you hear our news." They joined him at the kitchen table.

"Shoot," Donnie said.

Papa cleared his throat. "I still have friends at the university."

"I'm sure you do."

"I took the liberty of speaking to the head of the History Department. Charles Cowlson and I go back a long way. We were in the Faculty Senate together."

"Yes?" *Get to it,* Donnie thought impatiently.

"Charles is intrigued by your idea for a book on U.S.-Mexican relations."

"A book? I was just talking about research."

"No. It's a book. Trust me on that. Charles says he would welcome you back to the department."

"Now that the election's over and Payne's gone?" Donnie couldn't help it. He was cross.

"Hear me out. Charles said that he would welcome you back and that he would propose you as a scholar in residence at the National Autonomous University of Mexico in Mexico City. It's a two-year appointment. That should get you well along on your research."

Donnie sat up excitedly. "At UNAM? Is there a grant?"

"There's only a small stipend."

Donnie slumped back in his chair. "That lets me out then. I'm not taking money from either of you."

"That brings us to our second piece of news. Dorrie Louise has been organizing Lena's papers. Tell him, Dorrie Louise."

His mother's eyes shined brightly. "It's Lena's will. She has made some unusual arrangements."

Donnie listened, waiting for Dorrie Louise to get her thoughts in order.

"First of all, Papa, of course, is Lena's primary beneficiary. There seems to be enough to provide for him."

"That's good. And that's your money, Papa. Not mine."

"Just listen. She left the hotel and café to me." Dorrie Louise said excitedly. "Naturally, I agree to provide a home and a place where Papa can live and work for the rest of his life." She smiled fondly at Papa.

"That's wonderful," Donnie said. "You'll be a natural at keeping this place alive. It will be like Lena living on, in a way, through the Haven."

"That's it exactly, Donnie Ray," Dorrie Louise agreed, still excited.

"Hold on a minute. What about Grover?" The thought of Grover getting his hands on the Haven was too awful for Donnie to imagine.

Dorrie Louise smiled shyly. "I should have told you before, but I didn't want to worry you. Grover and I are divorcing."

"I'm astonished. When did this happen?"

"The decree just came through. We've been arguing about Grover's bird lands. He thinks I want them. Really all I want is for the girls to get their share of anything Grover comes into. He's agreed to give them half."

"Will that amount to anything?"

"I wouldn't be surprised. Grover's already thinking about how to approach the Braeswood people. He's decided that you and he are related, despite the divorce."

"Now that does not surprise me." Donnie grinned. He found Sid Banger's card in his pocket. "Tell Grover to call this man. He owes me a favor."

He looked at them and nodded with satisfaction. "That's all good, then. I can go out to Durango, save my money, and apply for the UNAM spot two years from now."

"There is one other matter." Dorrie Louise laid a paper covered with small print on the table. "There's this insurance policy. Lena took it out on her life when you first came here to live, in case anything happened to her. You're the beneficiary."

"It's not much," Papa said, "but with the university stipend, you should be able to live for two years in Mexico City."

"Really?" Donnie felt himself tearing up. "Lena. God bless her."

Papa stood and kissed Donnie's head. "Do good work, Donnie. That's what we want for you. That's what Lena would have wanted. Do good work."

"I will, Papa." He was quiet again. "There's just one thing missing."

"Yes, there is." Papa handed him a piece of paper with a phone number on it. "I also have this for you."

"What is it?"

"It's the telephone number of *Señorita* Cecilia Rueda Medina."

"How did you get this?"

"I called her father."

"Her father?"

"She didn't tell you that her father lived here for a year, when he was a student at the university? He writes us every year at Christmas. He had such good memories of his year here that he asked Lena to look after his daughter while she was at the law school. I called him to tell him of Lena's death. I told him a little about you and Cecilia. She has gone to work for a law firm in Mexico City. That's her number."

Donnie jumped up. "Tell Dr. Cowlson that I accept." He kissed them both. "Excuse me, but I have to go now."

"Where?" Papa asked.

"To buy a new cell phone…and a plane ticket."

THE END

About the Author

BOYD TAYLOR is a writer who lives in Austin, Texas. In his prior life, he was a lawyer and corporate manager.

Hero is the first book about the lives and times of Donnie Ray Cuinn. An erstwhile grad student in this book, his encounters with wrong-doers on both sides of the law, and his ill-fated romances, are continued in The Antelope Play and, most recently, in The Monkey House.

Boyd welcomes questions and comments from his readers. He can be contacted at www.boydtaylorauthor.com and followed on Facebook at: facebook.com/BoydTaylorAuthor

www.ingramcontent.com/pod-product-compliance
Lightning Source LLC
Chambersburg PA
CBHW022154260626
47155CB00018B/1895